PRAISE FOR P.D. SINGER

Fire on the Mountain —Rainbow Awards Jury's Choice Honorable Mention

"This was a well written, engrossing story and I can't wait to see where this series goes from here."
—Pants Off Reviews

"…a sexy and fun and sweet story."
—Under the Covers

Snow on the Mountain

"I highly recommend *Snow on the Mountain* to anyone who likes a romance mixed with misunderstanding, scandal, adventure, a little possessiveness, and a secret cabin in the mountains. It is as fun as it is sweet."
—Joyfully Jay

"…another treat from Ms. Singer and I really enjoyed it."
—Mrs. Condit Reads

Blood on the Mountain — Rainbow Awards Finalist, Honorable Mention (5*)

Read it for a cracking plot, and a wonderful couple that deserve their Happy Ever After.
—Mrs. Condit Reads

Snow on the MOUNTAIN

P.D. SINGER

ROCKY RIDGE BOOKS

Snow on the Mountain
Copyright © 2020 by P.D. Singer
Cover Art by Cosmic Letterz

Print ISBN: 978-1-62622-085-0

First edition Torquere Press 2009
Second edition Dreamspinner Press 2012

Published 2020 third edition

Rocky Ridge Books
Box 6922
Broomfield, CO 80021
http://RockyRidgeBooks.com

ALSO BY P.D. SINGER

For Eden, Meg, Julie, and Kim, who all said,
"You aren't stopping there, are you?"

Snow on the MOUNTAIN

ONE

The screams snapped my attention uphill. Nothing should have been happening behind my back. The skiers were supposed to sit still and let the chairlift take them to the top of the bunny slope. Quiet, other than the thrum of the machinery and the occasional conversation, was more usual. I was loading a munchkin-age ski class—they were wide-eyed and quieter than I expected. I'd slowed the lift to about half speed to seat them, which may have been all that saved that child.

A little girl shrieked and a second voice joined in, then more. "Do nothing fast" was really important now as I further slowed and then stopped the lift. Any quick motions would dislodge the small boy who now dangled upside down by one ski caught in the chairlift.

I knew how easily those bindings would release—I came out of mine every time I fell. A twist of an ankle would bring the child plummeting to the snow twenty feet below. His panicked thrashings made that more likely with every passing second.

"Jake, I call ski patrol!" yelled Egon, groping for the radio with his gloved hand. I hoped his accent wouldn't thicken beyond understanding from the tension, but he was already in the control hut and knew the channels. Have to learn those, but not in the middle of an emergency.

"Then come and help me!" I yelled back. I dashed into and out of the hut where Egon had been keeping watch. He barely noticed me scooping up the climbing rope and harness that he'd scolded me for even touching just a few days ago. The ski patrol did the rescues, he'd informed me snottily; the lowly lift operators were not to handle the equipment. I'd ignored him.

This kid couldn't wait for the patrol to show. Every second he stayed up was a gift from the heavens—he didn't have the minutes to spare for the experts. "Don't wiggle, kid! Hold real still! I'm coming up to get you!" I kept yelling at him to stop thrashing as I unraveled the coils. His chair had come to a halt about seventy yards from the loading area. I ran up the hill, glad for the packed snow under the lift.

I flung the rope up and over the cable, fully expecting to get elbowed out of the way. Whoever went up to fetch would only get there that much faster if the rope was already installed. The kid's hat fell on me. The kid might be next. I slung the end with the ascenders into position, feeding line and letting the weight of the hardware pull the rope over the cable. The other end of the rope had knots every few feet and would have fouled on the cable, something I would not have known if I hadn't scrutinized the equipment against Egon's wishes.

"Hold still, kid, we're coming!" I could see his wide, panicked eyes staring straight down at the unforgiving snow, which would snap his neck just as surely as concrete if he came out of that ski binding. The screaming from his seat partner and the kids in other chairs hadn't abated, though he was quiet now. There was no sign of the patrol—surely they'd be here in an instant? Egon appeared beside me, angling to be under the child to break his fall.

Where was the patrol? I had both ends of the rope together, so I shoved them at Egon. "Hold this taut! Tight!" His English was good, but.... The harness was attached to one jumar, the clip that stayed in one place with weight on it but would slide when unweighted. Where was the patrol? The kid was starting to shriek again, so I thrust my legs into the harness and brought the loose end around my waist to clip myself in.

Kurt had taught me to do this, though neither of us had ever envisioned the novice climber being the one to attempt a rescue. But it was me or Egon, who wasn't moving, and I knew I could get up that rope fast. "Keep it real tight. I'm going up!" I snarled at him. I grasped the doubled rope with my feet braced against the knots and jumared my hands up the other side. Kurt had emphasized safety over speed, but this kid's safety lay in speed. He could come down at any time. I was clipped in, that was as safe as it was going to get. I'd come down hard, too, if Egon couldn't keep enough weight on the rope. Maybe someone was down there helping him by now, but I dared not spend the attention to look.

"Hang on! I'm almost there," I kept reassuring the little boy and myself. A few more feet and I'd reach the chair. Hauling upward with my arms and pushing up with my feet on the knots was getting me where I needed to go. Little hands reached to me once I made it the last foot to chair level—I snagged the boy. He nearly strangled me with his arms around my neck. "I won't let you fall. I promise."

I could promise that now; it hadn't been a certainty at all. "We're going to go up a little more, okay?" I had to, or I wouldn't be able to get him unhitched. That damned binding should have released him with all the torque we were putting

3

on it, and it was stuck fast. I had no more hands available, so I hauled us up the rope with another few pulls of the jumars and clung for dear life with my feet, once I finally found one of the knots. He had U-turned as we went up and was upright again. I hoped he wouldn't pass out on me. "See, I got you," I crooned. I tried to decide how to get him untangled, now that the danger of a fall was past. At least he wasn't howling any more.

His ski was caught in the safety bar of the chair, but I had a second child to worry about while I fixed that. "Sweetie, you are going to sit real still while I lift the bar to get your friend unstuck, okay?" I tried to smile reassuringly at the little girl who had been uncorking the ear-splitting screeches. "All you have to do is sit real still." Suggesting that she might fall out if she didn't was a fast track to more screaming, I thought. She blinked at me and nodded a fraction of an inch. "Yeah, real still. Good, good...."

I felt like I was talking to one of the horses at the Rendezvous Lake Lodge stables, but the more I talked, the calmer she got, and the little guy who clung to me stayed still and quiet while I lifted the safety bar with one hand to release his ski. It swung around and finally came free, clipping me hard in the knee. The pain made me gasp, but I didn't drop anything or anyone. Now I wondered if I should take them both down. Where was the class instructor? They were wearing the number bibs of a ski school—more bibs were on the chairs ahead of us and on the one behind. The instructor was below me, apparently, along with a patrol, at last. I didn't want to get the kids, however frightened, separated from the rest of the group, but I wasn't the nanny on skis.

"Up or down?" I yelled.

"Up!" the instructor called back. "Go with them!" She

sprinted, or maybe clumped, back down to her skis, which she'd abandoned at the loading zone. "I'll meet you at the top!"

Of course I'd go with them. One screamer and one clinger would feel a whole lot better with an adult. No way was I was going to send two frightened children up the mountain alone.

"Looks like I get to ride with you guys!" I said with a brightness I didn't feel. "You sit down on this side, and I'll get in the middle." There would be just enough room if I didn't drop anyone getting in. The little boy let me put him in the lift chair and shifted his death grip from my neck to the chair arm. I was scared I'd tip the chair with my weight, but I was able to pull myself up one more arm's reach with the jumars and drop into the seat without altering the balance. The safety bar came down first, then I unclipped the harness from the rope. The kids seemed to approve of my priorities; they relaxed just a little, and the girl clutched the bar with her mittened hands.

"We're good!" I called down, and Egon, who had neither complained nor let go, began to haul the rope off the cable. He'd kept that rope taut, which must have taken his entire body weight, or the unanchored rope would have dropped me right out of midair.

"Wait for me at the top!" called the ski patrol, making my heart sink. I'd usurped his role in this rescue, certain that the child wouldn't remain dangling for long. I wondered how much trouble I was in.

That was going to have to wait while I chatted with my new buddies. By the time we got to the top of the mountain, they should be over the worst of their fright. I didn't want this event to spoil their perceptions of skiing, the way a broken ankle had spoiled mine.

The ride to the top let the kids relax; the little girl decided I was a good guy and snuggled up against me on the one side, and the little boy, cause of all this, wanted my arm over his shoulders. It was cold enough that I put my hat on him and hoped that the instructor had grabbed the one that had fallen on me. The lift started to move again, so I started asking questions, which got one-word answers at first. Soon they were yakking away as if nothing had ever happened, telling me their names, Gracie and Todd, that they were twins, five years old, almost six, and that they loved skiing more than anything.

We had a short way to the top when I asked the vital question. "Todd, what were you doing when you fell out?"

"See the pretties?" He pointed at the trees to either side of the lifts—people had thrown Mardi Gras necklaces into the branches. The trees were festooned in bright beads: purple, green, silver, gold. "Mama likes pretties, so I tried to get one for her. But they were too far away, and I fell out."

A child had nearly died for some festive trash. Such beads were common, Kurt told me when I'd asked, and I'd only thought it amusing. Now I wondered how many times I'd be shimmying up a rope, and if the child would end up clutching my waist or broken in the snow.

"They're too far away. I couldn't reach, and I've got grownup arms." I waved my arm out the side of the chair to demonstrate. "Promise you won't grab at them again?"

"Okay," he agreed with a mutinous pout. "But there was a close one."

"Not that close," I reminded him. He grinned at me, and I quit worrying about Todd no longer enjoying skiing and began to wonder more about what else he'd find to get into.

"Your job as a skier is to sit quietly on the chair until it's time to get off," I told them. "Which is now." I lifted the bar and helped them offload, help they probably didn't need, I thought enviously as they skied over to the little group of bibs who had already reached the top. They probably skied as well as I did; they could afford to be fearless because they didn't have nearly so far to fall. The instructor was a few chairs behind us, so I waited with the little group, none much bigger than my pals and none with ski poles.

Todd was done with me, but Gracie held my hand and chattered at the children, and when the instructor got to the top with the last of the kids, she introduced me.

"Miss Julie, this is Jake, he saved Todd, he's so cool!" All of this was getting recorded for posterity—I noticed a few people with their cell phones out taking pictures. Maybe videos. I didn't want to think about how many times my face would be on YouTube by tonight. One of the picture takers fell into a snow bank, and I couldn't bring myself to feel sorry for him.

Miss Julie checked Todd over carefully, though he was all agog to get back down the mountain and tried to squirm away. I checked out Julie: about my age, brunette curls exploding at the ends of long braids and a figure that looked all right even in insulated pants. Kurt had said the resort wanted good-looking employees. She looked like confirmation of his statement. If she always got the very young students, I was going to be seeing her a lot at the bunny slope lift.

"I guess he's okay. He's acting like his usual daredevil self," she said, swapping his blue hat with the big white pom-pom for my gray beanie. I was glad to get my head covered again, since my ears might freeze solid in another five minutes.

"I asked him if anything hurt, and he said no. More shaken than anything, and even that didn't last." I had to smile—Todd was scooting down the slope two feet at a time. He'd be at the foot of the mountain before this conversation was done if we didn't hurry. "He wanted to grab one of the necklaces in the trees for his mother."

"Figures," she said darkly. "His mother knows all about getting men to give her jewelry." I raised my eyebrows at her, and she squinched her face with embarrassment. "Did I say that out loud? Forget I said that, please." Her eyes carried a hint of flirtation.

Wondering who Todd's mother was, I just said, "Don't worry."

The ski patrol had off-loaded and had joined us. "Is the kid okay?" he asked Julie.

"The kid trying hardest to get away is the one who was upside down. He's fine, Mark." She spoke into her radio, and then she and her little crew were off to shouts of "Pizza slice turns! Follow me!" The line of tiny skiers, even Todd, trailed her across the snow doing snowplow turns, though Gracie had to hug me one last time before she followed the class, skiing with skill that none matched, except Todd.

The ski patrol introduced himself as Mark McAvoy and asked all the details of the rescue before he got to the question that worried me. "Why didn't you wait?" There was no anger in the question, making me think he only wanted to know, not that he wanted to admonish me.

"I knew how to use the equipment, and I thought the kid's ski was going to come off any second. It was about twenty feet down. I figured that I'd have the rope up for you, and then it didn't seem safe to wait any more."

"I'm glad you didn't, even if the lift operators aren't supposed to do that sort of thing. He could have come down at any minute. You were most of the way up the rope before I got there. I was halfway down the Galloping Goose; it took me a couple of minutes." That was an intermediate run, marked with a blue square on the maps, which led into the bunny hill.

I laughed, more at the name of the run than anything else.

This mountain had trails named everything from Helium Heights to Fast Track to Nowhere. The names at least told you exactly where you were, and it was a lot more fun to say "I fell twice on The Cereal Bowl," than "I fell twice on Easy Number Three."

"I figured you'd say something if I needed to know."

"I wasn't about to joggle your elbow, although you could have clipped the kid in with that extra webbing on the harness instead of your arm, but he was thin enough you could reach around him. You do some rock climbing?" Mark sounded friendly.

"Some. I've used jumars. Ascenders." Wish I'd realized about that extra strap; it might have saved me some worry.

"Good thing too." He made some notes in a pocket-sized notebook. "What's your full name? I'll need to put it in the report."

"Landon. Jake Landon."

"That's your alias today, Mr. Bond?" He smiled warmly, but I was rather proud of myself for performing some derring-do.

"I think I've got all the details, but what's your number if I need anything more?" He wrote it down and stuck the notebook into his pocket. "I'll see you round. There's a little pub that caters to the ski workers, not the tourists. Some of us get a beer there now and then. I could give you a call." He quirked an eyebrow, which disappeared into his hat.

"Thanks. I'm not much of a drinker, though." If the invitation was just friendly, and it included Kurt, then it might be nice to socialize with a group. We'd been hanging around home a lot since we'd come to Wapiti Creek because we weren't entirely clear on how to handle ourselves in public. Did we introduce each other as partners, roommates, friends? How out did we want to be?

Mark waved and skied down the hill, making it look like the easiest thing in the world. I headed back to the off-loading ramp and sat in a freshly emptied chair to get whirled around the big pulley and toted back down the hillside. On the way down, I considered the casual way Mark had basically asked me out. I wasn't used to that, by a long shot. He was as tall as I was and a lot more athletic, certainly more socially poised. Kind of good-looking, with brown hair long enough to escape his wool hat, and wide, sensuous lips. But he wasn't Kurt, so I didn't want anything more from him than some friendship.

On the trip down, I wondered if Kurt was worried about me looking elsewhere.

TWO

"So, the hero returns?" Egon razzed me when I got off the chairlift.

"Shut up, you idiot," I responded pleasantly, though I didn't like him much. He had an assortment of grudges and was usually surly, but I'd conceived a hope that his attitude might adjust as a result of this little adventure. If he thought I was going to play lone hero over this, he was mistaken, because that would only grow another grudge, this one personal. "That kid needed both of us."

He'd been tending the chairlift base alone while I'd gone up and come down, which gave him time to have all sorts of conversations in his head. Maybe what I said wasn't what he'd been telling himself, because he squinted at me over the heads of a couple of ten-year-olds who trudged up to the loading zone with their snowboards.

"Seriously. I could not have climbed that rope if you hadn't been holding on. So cut the hero talk." I spoke into the clear space as the chair yanked the two boys into the air. "We were a team." I paused while a couple of women in expensive ski clothing shuffled to the loading zone. The chair hauled them and their appraising glances away before I spoke again. "And thanks for not dropping me."

He sniffed. "I would not drop you unless I was sure you land on your thick head." He grinned. "Your head is thick—you must know that only your part in this rescue will be noticed by the people, who will be watching on Internet by tonight, if not already."

My heart sank. A couple came up to the loading zone, a man who looked experienced and a woman who looked nervous. "Just let the chair sit you down as it comes up behind you," he coached her, buying me some time to think what to say. It was good advice, though she sat with a flump and a yip, leaving me to respond to Egon.

"Doesn't matter," I finally said. "I know it took both of us."

Those words were barely out of my mouth when I got grabbed and kissed.

She didn't let go fast enough, so when the chair came up behind her, the upright clipped me hard on the ear. Her forward motion dragged me a couple of steps up the hill before she released her grip on my jacket. The damage was done—I'd been pulled off balance and landed with a splat on the snow. Egon didn't even try not to laugh, the jerk, but he didn't drown out what she was calling back over her shoulder.

"Sorry! I'll be back to do it right! But you saved that kid!"

Aggh. I did not want to be kissed by any more presumptuous little rich girls. Her seat partner yelled, "I get to kiss you too!" That made Egon laugh even harder. I picked myself off the snow with all the dignity I could muster.

"See? No one offers me kisses," he gloated.

"Kiss off," I muttered, brushing myself off. "I'll be in the control hut for a while." I could hide there and still do my job while this nine-day wonder died down. Hope it didn't take nine days.

I had been on the job for several days, but had spent little time in the control hut. I'd been mostly helping people load and unload on the bunny lift. The beginners spent their days on this gentle slope, learning the basics of controlling their equipment, or in the case of the super shredder preteens, scaring the beginners with their snowboard antics.

This early in the season it wasn't crowded. Most of the mountain had only been opened in the last day, after a storm had come across and dropped just over a foot of snow. The groomers had been out all night, driving the snowcats over the wider trails. The narrower trails were still being curried into skiability with the smaller, snowmobile-pulled drags. Almost all the easy, or green slopes, and most of the blue intermediate trails were finished, but several of the expert trails, the black diamonds and double diamonds, would be left as powder. It would be a miracle if they could groom the double diamonds, even with winches, since I didn't know how anyone, even Kurt, could ski those and live.

The mountain was getting busier as the season advanced. Opening day this year had been earlier than last year between snowmaking efforts and the gift from nature, but most people hadn't planned to be here so soon. That might keep my face off the Internet. I could hope. It could have been worse. It could have happened next weekend, over Thanksgiving, when the crowds would be substantially larger.

It could get worse now. I saw my boss, Roy, talking with Egon, who pointed him toward the hut with an evil smile.

"Audition for the Ski Patrol today, Jake?" Roy asked when he'd joined me in the control hut.

"That's not why I did it, sir." I did not want him to think I was grandstanding with this.

"Tell me what happened," he asked, so I did, leaving out nothing.

"The kid is just fine?" he asked again when I finished.

"He couldn't wait to make the next run." My little buddies Gracie and Todd had waved happily from the chairlift twice already.

"No harm done, then. Do you have another parka?"

I looked down at the light gray with black slashes. "Yes, why?"

"Wear it to work tomorrow and plan on working the upper end of the lift. I don't think the Denver news stations will get teams up here before then. We aren't going to make it easy for them to turn this into a news story. Some sharp lawyer is going to see that a kid nearly fell, not that the kid was saved." He looked irritated. "Then they'll try to regulate the industry some more."

I'd wear my other hat and different sunglasses too. I didn't relish the idea of microphones getting shoved into my face. I might say something that would trigger a huge lawsuit. "What about the parents?" I didn't know what they'd be told or who was supposed to tell them. Please don't let it be me.

"Todd and Gracie's folks aren't going to sue the resort, Jake."

I wondered how he was so certain, but his confidence was infectious. He smiled and thumped my shoulder. "They'd have your head if you'd dropped him, but you didn't. Good job on that, Jake. Really good. Now let's keep the publicity to a minimum."

I almost broke my neck nodding agreement to that. "If

there's a light bulb changer or something really long, we can get the beads out of the trees, not tempt some other kid." Besides, I knew who might like to have some.

"Good idea, but just take down the close ones, or we'll have more getting flung. I'll send someone out." He warned me again not to speak to the press and headed to the warming hut. Some hut: antler chandeliers, fieldstone fireplaces, fancy food and designer goggles for sale, but traditional names just stuck.

"Finished hiding, hero?" Egon asked when I came back with a pocket full of "pretties."

"No, I just figured you'd want to go sit down in the control hut again, wuss." Whatever truce we'd had was holding. We were bantering and not snarling.

Egon was here from Bulgaria on a cultural exchange visa, which made him eligible for jobs where he'd interact with the public, on the theory that he'd teach people something about his culture. So far I hadn't learned a thing about Bulgaria, other than it was an up-and-coming ski area for Europe and that Bulgarians could be just as cranky as Americans about being passed over for jobs.

He'd made that perfectly plain this morning when Kurt had come by the bunny run with a young woman, my age or maybe a year or two younger, and noticeably more adept on her skis than most of the folks lining up to ride this lift. He gave me a great big grin, and no wonder he was pleased: on his first day teaching with the Alpenschlössl Ski School, his client wasn't a beginner as rank as his other private student—me. He'd probably have some fun as part of the lesson, not just basic instruction and picking her up off the snow.

He'd looked great in his red parka and black pants, only the flapping lift ticket and the discreet "Alpenschlössl" pin looked different from an ad for overpriced ski clothes.

"Hey, Jake!" He and his student shuffled far enough up to catch the chairlift. "We're going to practice some skills before heading to the steeper slopes." He winked before the chair carried them away.

"Alpenschlössl instructors don't usually teach that age bracket." Egon's voice was snide.

"Really? How would you know?" I slowed the lift to let a couple of little kids get on safely, then brought the safety bar down before they got out of reach. Egon sped the lift again before replying.

"Oh, the whole mountain knows. They hire only the best, you see." I turned in surprise at the degree of venom he was showing. "They were going to hire me, until this other man interviewed." He jerked his thumb viciously uphill toward Kurt. "Suddenly they had no need for me, though I had all but signed the contract."

"That's too bad." Somehow, this hadn't seemed like the right time to tell Egon that he was jerking his thumb at my lover. "So the kids don't need that caliber of instructor?"

"Hah. The parents take such instructors for themselves." With that bit of rancor, Egon had stomped back to the control hut, leaving me feeling proud of my lover for being acknowledged as one of the best and wondering how I was going to get along with someone who hated Kurt for being just that much better than he.

I was glad Egon had more or less gotten over his snit before Todd toppled.

Late in the afternoon, I found my little buddies just outside the lift line. Motioning to Egon to take the loading deck, I headed over to them. When Gracie saw me, she started to wave wildly and shriek. At least it was happy shrieks this time.

"Jake! Jake! Come tell my mama!"

Oh, great, even if lawsuits were as unlikely as Roy seemed to think, I didn't want to tell the person with enough clout to retaliate that her darling child nearly had a fatal accident today. Mama was a lovely, well-groomed brunette, who looked like late twenties but could have been older, in a spandex ski suit that I recognized from my outfitting as costing rather more than I was going to make this month.

Her companion was someone I recognized too: Ulf, Kurt's fellow and least favorite colleague at the Alpenschlössl Ski School. I'd decided he had muscles in his forehead when I'd met him, and his attitude hadn't improved much when he'd come by with students. He looked disdainfully at me and went for "ignore" this time. I returned the favor.

"Hi, Gracie. Heya, Todd." Gracie had flung herself at me, so "Todd" came out more like "oof." "Hey, buddy, I brought you something." Using one hand to helplessly pat my little admirer and the other to dig the beads out of my pocket, I smiled apologetically. "Excuse me, ma'am...." That got me a glower, like she thought I should have said "miss," but her children were hanging all over me. "Here you go, I took care of it." I handed Todd the necklaces in a way that was bound to spoil the boy's surprise but avoid arousing her suspicions that I was doing something nefarious.

"Oooh! Thank you, Jake!" Todd left off yanking on my jacket and turned to his mother. "Mama! This is for you!" She looked puzzled at the waving strings of green and gold, but she did finally lean down to let him hang the beads around her neck. "Jake helped me get the pretties for you!"

That made Ulf turn around and look daggers at me. What was his problem?

"Thank you, Toddy. Thank you, Jake." She gave me a sideways look. "How did you three become so friendly, may I ask?"

Gracie started to yammer out the whole story, but I figured I'd better get my version out first and spoke over her, patting her to quiet. "He got a little tangled up in the chairlift trying to get some beads, so I untangled him, and we rode to the top of the hill together." True, if incomplete. "They've been waving to me every time they get on the chair since then. They're very nice kids." I smiled, hoping that the compliment would distract her; she seemed like the sort who'd use her children for stylish accessories.

"Thank you," she said dismissively.

Recognizing my cue to get lost, I told the kids I had to get back to the lift and left them chattering with Mama about what to do next. "Come ski with us, Mama! Come see how good we're getting!"

I saw the group next in the short lift line, arguing about who would ride with whom. "Sit with me, Mama!"

"No, me!"

"You will sit together this time." Commanding.

"I wanna sit with you!" Mutinous.

"We can sit all three! Jake sat with both of us!" Oh no, I did not want to become involved in this family drama, and they were about three pairs back of the head of the line now.

"No, we are not sitting all three. Gracie, Todd, you will ride together. Ulf and I will sit together. End of discussion." She sounded cold. Poor kids, they just wanted her attention.

They were at the head of the line now. The adults waited about fifteen feet back of the loading zone as the kids slid to the mounting mark. I slowed the lift to let the kids load and get the bar down, which gave Todd enough time to grumble to me, "I hate Ulf. He takes Mama away all day."

Mama and Ulf loaded without a glance at me, though Ulf exchanged some sort of lifted eyebrow communication with

Egon, who stood on the other side of the loading zone. I watched them swing into the air. Their skis had barely left the snow before Ulf pulled the bar down and put his arm over her shoulder; she snuggled into him. When I glanced up the hill again, it was in time to see her arm flash out, releasing green and gold twinkles to land in the trees.

THREE

Good cooking smells greeted me on the way through the door of our one-bedroom apartment in employee housing. It was little, but it was home, because that's where Kurt was waiting for me.

"Going to have to lay off the garlic, Jake. Last night's dinner got me yelled at this morning." He came out of the kitchen to kiss me. He must've caught an earlier shuttle home and gotten dinner started, which meant that any garlic issues tomorrow were on him. He'd peeled down to his long underwear, top and bottom, which clung to his lithe body and looked pretty comfy for lounging around.

"Really? You don't taste garlicky to me." I probed his mouth with my tongue, trying to find a reason for his boss to be upset. "And why was he close enough to notice?"

"You had just as much spaghetti as I did; you wouldn't notice." Kurt was tasting me just as completely—at this rate, dinner might burn before we established whether or not the garlic bread had overstayed its welcome. "Rudi was vetting me before sending me out on a *zur Burg* lesson. Top-of-the-line package, and I didn't make the grade. Sucky way to start a new job. Amber said the tips from those are good. Ulf was already booked, so Rudi ended up with it. And he was pissed with me."

"That's too bad. I saw who Ulf was booked with. Money and two kids." Ulf had seemed awfully comfortable with her too, judging from the snuggling in the chairlift. I made a note to lay off the garlic since Kurt, who had never acted concerned about money before, seemed interested in making as much as possible. If it mattered to him now, I wouldn't do things that interfered. Most of my pay went to the tuition savings account, but that wasn't Kurt's responsibility.

"Yeah. But they all have to have bucks to pay Alpenschlössl rates." The ski school Kurt just hired on with had the highest rates and the best ski instructors at the Wapiti Creek Resort. They also had the best-looking instructors on the mountain.

Kurt certainly qualified on that score; he was about five feet ten, with a slim but muscular build, shoulders broadened from swinging axes and shovels, and quite possibly the nicest ass on the planet, but then, I'm biased. He'd let his blond hair grow longer than he'd kept it all summer, when we'd both trimmed short for life in the mountains without running water. Now it was curling over his ears and forehead, nearly the same shade as his well-defined features, still tanned from our summer in the Uncompahgre National Forest. His eyes, the brilliant blue of the Colorado sky, made a startling contrast, which I liked to explore from kissing range.

He was also a fine instructor for a lot of skills, something that I could personally attest to. Since meeting him, I'd learned to shoot a bow and arrow, ride a horse, rock climb, and cook on a propane stove. I'd taught him to fish, though he didn't have enough patience to enjoy it the way I did. He was also teaching me about being one half of a couple, and that was best of all.

But Kurt had been shoveling snow, not teaching, the sort of pick-up job he could get after the lifts opened. We'd painted hotel rooms in the gap season, but the smell of wet paint was no longer welcome once the guests began to arrive in earnest. I'd already been tending the bunny lift for a week.

Kurt had turned down one teaching job for not paying enough, and while his assurances of getting hired without a problem hadn't dwindled, he was beginning to show a little strain around the eyes. So when I came home last night to find him pulling on fleece and microfiber for an interview, I knew he had really high hopes for the Alpenschlössl Ski School.

"How do I look?" Kurt held out his arms, twisting his shoulders to mimic a fashion model. "He said to dress like I would for teaching."

I looked him up and down, from the high-tech boots and ski pants, to the fleece shirt over the silky turtleneck of some wonder fabric, all in black and red. "You look great. The clients will be all over you." I was afraid of that.

"I can fend them off, just so long as you are all over me." He grinned and stepped forward for a kiss. I grabbed his ass and smooched him.

"I'd be all over you anyway."

"Good." He grabbed my butt with one hand and then swatted it gently. "But let's get this interview over with first."

I drove him to the interview in silence. This was the ski school that had wanted pictures with his résumé. I'd thought that was weird, but he'd reassured me that it was a sneaky way to get around some labor laws. In a place that catered to the rich and the famous who thought the likes of Aspen too ordinary, they wanted good-looking staff, and he hadn't quibbled about it.

I parked between an Escalade and a Beemer SUV, feeling like the crudmobile was way out of place. "For luck." I squeezed Kurt's hand, then watched him climb the two steps into the Alpenschlössl Ski School office. I'd wait for him out here.

Unfortunately, the late afternoon was blustery, cold, and getting dark. The crudmobile leaked chilly air at the gaskets, which probably wouldn't keep it from killing me with carbon monoxide if I kept the motor idling, so I went into the Alpenschlössl office and sat down next to the magazine rack. The receptionist winked at me when I told her I was only waiting for Kurt. She went back to looking at her magazine, and then answered the phone. The rates she quoted for a ski lesson package made me extra glad Kurt would teach me for the joy of it, because the figure sounded a lot like our monthly rent.

The young woman, who was blonde, attractive, and inclined to chew her fingernails—I love Kurt, but I do notice, okay?—was sitting behind a dark wood desk, ski posters of places like Banff, Chamonix, and Flaine on the walls behind her. There was a door to her left, where, I assumed, Kurt and his prospective boss were hashing out the details.

A tall blond man in ski clothes entered while she was still on the phone and took a seat on her desk, one thigh raised against the edge. He scowled at the closed door, then at me. What? I was just waiting.

"Did Rudi not decide upon Egon?" His words were to her, but his sneer was to me. "Or does he want corn-fed Americans now?"

She slapped his thigh. "Be nice, Ulf. He's just waiting for his buddy."

"Asshole." I kept it to half volume to make my opinion felt

without escalating the situation. He didn't get up off the desk. Kurt wouldn't have to spend much time around this guy, I hoped.

The door opened to let Kurt through, and he looked mad. He noticed me when I stood up to follow him out the door. "Say, Jake. Are you a happy man?"

He had to be asking for the benefit of the tall man in his mid-thirties who was right on his heels.

"Yes, Kurt, I am a happy man," I said. What the hell was this about? It wasn't like any job interview I'd ever had.

"Are you agreeable to Kurt taking this job?" the ski school manager asked me.

Weirder and weirder. "I'm sitting here waiting for him, aren't I?"

Rudi nodded thoughtfully. "You can start tomorrow. I'm sure Amber has some bookings for you already. Amber also teaches, and this is my other instructor, Ulf Seiler. Let's take care of the employment contract." He disappeared into the office. Kurt looked at me, shrugged, and followed him.

This "Ulf" jerk swung his leg back and forth, thudding against the desk, alternately glaring at the closed door and at me. "How unusual," he sneered in some European accent, "to meet a happy man."

Before I'd decided how to respond to that, Kurt returned, in a better mood than before, waving a yellow paper and a key.

"Let's hit the road, Jake!"

Fine with me—it got us out from under Ulf's unpleasant stare. I held the door for him, listening to his good news. "I'm employed, you're employed, the snow is fresh; life is good!"

I'd asked him later if he'd read that contract through thoroughly before he signed it, and he'd said only that it looked okay. That meant he hadn't. I'd have to read it over and see if there were any dangerous clauses in there. I hoped I could recognize the dangerous clauses.

I wanted to hear about his first student, the upper slopes, and most of all, I wanted to let him bask in a new job that he'd hoped to have nailed two weeks ago. He had to be relieved and he'd earned the gloat.

Once I'd pulled off layers down to my long johns, we sat down to eat chili and cornbread. "Whoops!" My bowl of chili slid toward the edge. The table leg had buckled again when I caught it with a foot.

"I'll brace the joint," Kurt said, "or you're going to be wearing more of my good cooking." I flinched at the memory of the hot stew that had been much better in my belly than it had been in my lap.

"I'll do it." I should have done it before, since I'd lived with this crummy folding table and knew its habits. One day, I thought, I'd have a nice sturdy oak table that I could trust to hold my plate. "Tell me about your day?"

"The girl you saw me with this morning wanted to spend a lot of time on moguls, so we went up top to Killy's Knees. She really improved a lot. Bet her legs are like rubber tonight." He laughed. "I had to tire her out enough that she'd quit getting lovey on the lifts, so I ran her through the bumps for about an hour and a half. That was just weird; she kept scooting over at me until I stuck my elbow in her ribs."

That put a catch in my throat, which I had to swallow down, reminding myself that he had sharp elbows and had used them.

"Hey, I got kissed today." I might as well tell him the worst. "And I have a girlfriend now."

Two or three beans went down the wrong hatch at that— Kurt finally managed to hack out, "You what?" once I'd thumped his back a couple of times.

"Yup. The one who kissed me thought I was a hero for getting a little boy off the lift before he fell, but she dumped me fast." I filled in the rest of the details, starting with the rescue and ending with me on my butt in the snow, while he went from disbelief to pride to laughter. "And my girlfriend, Gracie, is five years old."

"Five? Jake! What are you going to do with a five-year-old?" Kurt snorted.

"I don't know, go skiing with her? Except she probably skis better than I do." I chewed a bite of chili glumly.

"Think I need to give you another lesson." Kurt's grin was impish, making me think of all the lessons he might hand out. He swirled some butter on a piece of cornbread and licked his lips.

"Thing is, the publicity could get pretty intense on this. My boss is freaked out about it."

"Suppose so. Hey, I'm just glad we did so much climbing last summer." He smiled at me, making my heart stop. We'd spent time on the scarp while he taught me rock climbing, but that was after we'd spent time in a cave in the scarp, waiting for the fire that we thought would kill us and hoping to survive. We'd become lovers that night, though it had taken a while to straighten out the details. It had made the rest of our season as forest rangers in the mountains of Colorado into a whole new kind of heaven.

That blinding smile made the dimple near the right corner of his mouth show; I loved that dimple. Actually, what I loved was Kurt—charming, confident, competent Kurt Carlson, who, at twenty-five, was good at so many things I could barely do or had never tried. He was teaching me a lot of those skills, and had assured me that I'd be good at them, too, by the time I was twenty-five. I had a lot to perfect in the next two and a half years.

Maybe by then I'd have mastered my heart too, and not be so scared of this relationship. It was still amazing to me that he wanted me as much as I wanted him, that he cared for me as much as he did. We'd been lovers for the five months since the fire, and if I was really lucky, we'd be together always.

An attractive, capable guy like Kurt could have anyone he wanted, and he wanted me. While we were rangers, there hadn't been much competition; we could go for days not seeing other humans. In a town like Wapiti Creek, where beautiful people were thick on the ground, I could only hope that our bond was strong enough to stand up to everyone who would find him appealing. I certainly loved him, and I thought he loved me, though we'd never said those words out loud. It had been hard enough to get past the barriers in our heads to become lovers.

Maybe I was just going to have to make that stretch. This new environment was testing us; I wanted to feel as secure with him in town as I did in the wilderness. We'd already scared each other once tonight with stories of other people, and I hadn't even mentioned Julie or Mark. Hearing the words would do wonders for my confidence, but if I wanted to hear them, I'd have to be willing to say them.

Kurt caught me cleaning up the kitchen. "Mmmmm, in those long johns, you look ready for a ski lesson." He snuggled up behind me, his legs pressed against mine from ankle to butt, his cock snugged against my ass, his strong arms pulling my back against his chest.

"How, in the kitchen?" I rubbed my ass against him, feeling how his cock was rising. Two layers of high tech fabric were going to have to come off soon.

He was kissing the back of my neck, which was going to make me start dropping dishes. "I am a damned good instructor, so there should be a way. In fact—" He shifted his feet so they were parallel with mine, his body totally plastered against me. "—I don't think I would use this approach with just any student, but...."

I could feel his cock pressed to my crack. "You better not!" I decided to wash the chili pot, since I couldn't do more than dent it. His hands on my hips excited me.

"Shhh! You have to feel the balance like this." Kurt began to sway his hips gently from side to side, moving me. "You want to turn, you shift your weight like this." His knees against mine made me shift my balance. "You unweight, then once you're around, you shift back, you weight again." He shifted me the other way. "Now let's turn the other direction." Again he changed my balance; his warm breath on my neck made me decide to put the pot down before it made a clatter. "See?" We "turned" several times as he coached me, and now that my hands were free, he took them, sliding under my forearms so that we were holding each other and some phantom ski poles. My own growing erection rubbed against the edge of the counter in front of the sink.

"Yeah, this is lots of fun. Keep turning. Mmmm." He laid his cheek against my back as we "skied" through the kitchen, though my own preferred terrain at this point was in the bedroom, covered with burgundy-striped sheets rather than snow. "You're doing good, Jake, not one fall. Keep going. You're going to kick ass tomorrow." His shoulders angled slightly when we shifted weight, turning me, getting me into the rhythm. I did my best to follow his movements. Desire was warring with understanding that I really was doing the correct motions. "Yeah, shift your weight to the left, now come back up. Practice it slow, then speed it up for the slopes. Bend your knees."

Damn, how did Kurt come up with so many ways to drive me crazy? He'd just thought of a fresh one.

"We need a ski pole now." He nibbled on the back of my neck, then pushed me over the sink and pulled my long johns down.

"What?" I tried to look at him over my shoulder, seeing his smiling face and then his arm snaking over to take a glob of butter out of the dish. He had one hand on my back, holding me down while he wiped the butter into my ass, plunging two slippery fingers in as I tried to relax for him. Tonight wouldn't be a "lot of foreplay" night, but that was fine—I was plenty worked up from our "ski runs" and groaning from his fingers slithering in and out. He checked my hole one last time before pulling his own long johns down just enough for what I knew he was going to do. "Ski pole, huh?" I gasped as he pushed into me.

"You bet!" Kurt laughed deep in his throat and pulled me back upright against him. "Don't lose the balance." His hips continued their slow skiing twists; his arms held me tight, so I followed, feeling how he slipped in and out of me as we slalomed in the kitchen. His hands were flat against my chest as he writhed. I could only hold him with my hands on his hips. The skiing was getting lost, but the wonderful feeling of his cock working in and out of me slowly carried me along. I stayed slow as best I could in our excitement, and then to hell with it.

"Moguls ahead," I told him, and then picked up the pace, slamming back against him without trying to "turn." I knew the big bumps on the slopes needed fast reactions, even if I had no hope of negotiating them for real.

"Whoo! Moguls!" With a soft bite to my neck, Kurt bent me over into the sink and thrust into me fast. One hand on my shoulder pulled me back against him, and then he leaned over me, reaching forward to grasp my hard, thick cock. I yelled out, loving the way he pumped my cock. His strong hand moved at about twice the pace of his hips, speeding me toward the finish line. I had a hold on his ass with one hand, though I needed the other to keep me from falling into the soapy water in the sink as we raced toward climax. This slope we were negotiating was high and steep; on this mountain, I could do the double black diamonds.

He filled me and pulled away before plunging back into my ass, sure of his terrain, equally sure how to touch me in front, letting me thrust into his fist. My climax built inside. Kurt doubled over flat to my back and pulled me onto his cock; he held me there as he groaned, paralyzed from his climax. My own was nearly there—I couldn't bear not to go over the precipice, no matter how I loved to feel Kurt pulsing within me. My hand on his, together we stroked my shaft those few last times to take me over that last jump until my orgasm caught air.

It was a while before I could turn around to hold him, and I damn near fell into the soapy water trying to stand upright. He was breathing as hard as I was, and only then did I think to shut off the open tap.

Now would be a good time to tell him that I loved him. Except I didn't want him to think that all I meant was that the sex was great, though it was. I should tell him.

I slipped my tongue gently between his lips, more of a caress than a kiss. "Wonderful run, Kurt."

FOUR

The evenings were different without any of the diversions we'd used all summer—it was too cold and dark for archery; there was no lake to swim in, though if we wanted to, we could go over to the gym and work out. Kurt had explained that we'd have to use it sooner or later, now that he wasn't shoveling snow to work his upper body, and I wasn't getting enough exercise period, standing all day at the lift. I thought getting up from repeated falls was enough exercise, but I knew that as I got better, I'd need more upper body work too. Funny how many muscles get used to haul yourself upright with a pair of ski poles.

Lately, we'd been watching some television, reading, or surfing the Internet when we weren't jumping each other's bones, though that was by far my favorite way to spend the evening. When I'd complained about the television, Kurt had suggested taking up the bagpipes. That led to me knocking him over on the couch, sucking his pipe and groping his bag to demonstrate the only acceptable way to play bagpipes indoors. He'd cooperated to the extent of making horrid Scottish noises while I played him, but that wasn't going to work tonight, and we weren't sleepy yet. I'd almost resigned myself to letting him turn on the television when the phone rang.

"Hey, Jake? It's Mark. A bunch of us are over at McTavish's, playing darts. You want to come?"

I asked Kurt what he thought, because I wasn't going to lead Mark on just to get some social life. Mark was part of the story I hadn't told Kurt yet, mostly because I wasn't sure that there was any story there to tell, though this same-day phone call made me think harder about it. "A bunch of us" sounded innocuous and more than enough to cover another player. If we came together, Mark should get the "just friends" part without me ever having to tell him "sorry, no thanks."

"That will be fun!" Kurt's eyes lit up, giving me the sinking feeling that here was another of those things he could do like a champ, while I was a mediocre player at best. Maybe I could get a backgammon board somewhere; that was something I was good at.

"Sounds good. We'll see you in a bit." I hung up without explaining the "we" part, though I reminded Kurt that Mark was the ski patrol. "We really haven't gone anywhere since we've been here. The wallets should stand it." A lift operator didn't make a whole lot, nor had I seen my first paycheck of the season, though I'd saved most of my ranger's pay.

"Depending on how skilled the dart players are, the wallet should come home fatter than it left!" Kurt kissed me with considerable glee. Yup, he had to be a good darts player, especially since he had a wealth transfer in mind. Probably went with the archery skills; he was Robin Hood personified. I might be better at it than I remembered, too, since he'd turned me into an approximation of Will Scarlet. "Go get ready!"

There were some ways that a town life was really fine. Like a hot shower any time I wanted. I jumped in while Kurt fiddled with the remote control on the TV. It sounded too loud to me after the quiet of the mountains, with no sounds beside our own voices, the rumble of the tank truck, and the birds, insects, animals, and wind. Also the occasional roar of a forest fire, but I didn't miss that at all. I stuck my head into the spray to rinse out the shampoo and drown out the sounds of Hollywood in a box.

I toweled off, watching myself in the mirror, looking for whatever it was Kurt saw in me. My reflection showed a young man with brown hair and brown eyes, six feet tall, with the physique of someone who worked for his exercise instead of getting it at the gym. The extra pizza pounds had been left behind in the wilderness months ago—I couldn't resist flexing a bicep just to see the ripples under my skin.

Kurt leaped into the tiny shower, and I stood in front of the sink with a razor. I glanced at the outline behind frosted glass, happy to be going out with him, worried that we really hadn't discussed how to behave. It hadn't been a problem during the ranger season, since most of the time we were around other people there was something unromantic going on, like a forest fire.

On our forays into town, we assumed it was a case of "turn your calendar back twenty years" on the attitude, so we didn't walk closely at the grocery store or hold hands on the street. That was actually fine with me, because I was all over Kurt in private but not at all sure I wanted to be open in public.

Wapiti Creek was probably as cosmopolitan a place as could be found in the mountains, but I still wasn't ready to walk into the pub with one hand on Kurt's shoulder. "Guess we should play it cool, huh?"

"We can, if you want." Kurt turned serious eyes on me. *There's no "should" about it,* I read within their depths.

"Kurt, you know that...." This was heading into uncertain territory, so I showed him, lips to lips, what he ought to know. "But let's not do any public displays of affection yet, okay?"

"Yet." Kurt slipped me some tongue before pulling away to swab himself with the towel. "Since we didn't even ping each other's gaydar all that well at first, I think we'll do okay." Kurt had spent two weeks trying to get my attention, which he'd gotten all right, though it had taken me a lot longer and a fairly direct invitation before I could believe that was happening.

But now I knew.

And if Mark had really asked me out, the only person I was fooling with the closet act was me.

At the other end of a shuttle ride into what passed for downtown, we found McTavish's, a pleasant pub with some pool tables, a couple of dartboards, and tables for small groups in the rest of the space. It was pretty full, and the cheery sound of Irish fiddles was entwined in the happy babble, some of which came out of a television mounted near the ceiling.

I looked around for Mark, who spotted me and waved. Kurt followed me around the edge of the darts alley while I tried to identify any of the other people. Some looked familiar from lift lines, but the only other face I had a name for was Julie. Egon was across the room with another group. I hoped he'd stay there.

"Hi, Jake!" Mark's face stayed steady as he took in my companion. "Hi, I'm Mark."

"Kurt. Jake said you guys were playing darts tonight, so I came along." Kurt smiled at him, and then we tried to keep names and faces straight. The other seven or eight people in the group were introduced in a hodgepodge of "Charlie, Marty,

Julie, Kim, Devon, Chelsea, Gabe, Dave." I interrupted being identified as "the guy who rescued the kid" by decamping for the bar with Mark while Kurt and Devon went to round up another couple of chairs.

The pints of beer I ordered for me and Kurt would have to last me the evening. When I said I wasn't much of a drinker, I meant it. I'd left that behind in Boulder, or perhaps I should say I'd left it in Glenwood Springs on that messy road trip with my college friends. Weekend parties and getting stupid had lost their allure and had sent me running into the mountains. Kurt and I had had maybe one six-pack between us the entire summer, and that had led to some foolish behavior. We'd tried having sex in a canoe, an unstable, unforgiving platform for vigorous movement. The canoe had punished us by dropping us in the cold, cold lake just before we'd finished. No, no large amounts of beer for Jake tonight. The social lake could be just as cold.

"So, is he a friend from before or someone you met on the mountain?" Mark asked while we waited for the bartender to pour.

"We did a ranger season together." Honesty without particulars seemed like the way to go. I wouldn't deny Kurt, but I didn't want to explain in detail either.

He nodded. I could see the gears turning in his head: ranger season, followed up here, came out on what might have been a date, cha-ching. "So you came tonight because…?" Yeah, he'd really asked me out. I hate being a social moron sometimes.

"Because a guy needs friends." Well, we'd gotten it out in the open right away, and he didn't need to hear details to get it. When we carried the beer back to the tables, Mark walked just a little bit farther away than when we'd gone to the bar. Kurt accepted the drink with a smile and went back to chatting with Julie and Kim.

The conversation flowed around the table, making it clear that some of the group knew each other, while others were as new as we were, so the subjects went all over the map. I put together that Julie, Chelsea, and Dave were instructors, Devon worked the ski rentals, Mark, Marty, and Kim patrolled, Gabe had one of the high mountain lifts that serviced the expert slopes, and whatever Charlie did on the mountain, he was miscast because he should have been a fricking gossip columnist.

Kurt and Dave were just getting up to play a round of darts when Charlie started dropping his little bombshells. "Hey, Jake, that kid on the bunny lift today—you know who he is?"

"Todd." I hadn't asked his last name, though the boy and his sister had volunteered everything else under the sun.

"Underwood." Mark took a sip of his drink.

I listened to this with one eye on Kurt, who had his back to us, throwing one dart after another. "Meaning…?"

"His daddy owns the controlling interest in Wapiti Creek and about four other big resorts, not to mention developing all those million-dollar condos. So, that was, like, the boss's kid." A shudder ran around the table at Charlie's explanation.

That shouldn't matter, I told myself; I didn't know that when I went up the rope to get him, and he was safe now. Still, I felt cold just knowing. I glanced over at Julie, who looked at me with sad understanding. She'd known—no wonder she'd nearly wet herself today.

"That explains why their mama looks like quite the trophy." I thought back to the elegant but icy brunette. "She was skiing with an instructor."

That news dimmed Charlie's toothpaste commercial grin. "It wasn't Ulf from Alpenschlössl, was it?"

"I think so, why?"

Charlie shook his head slowly, like it hurt. "Melanie has no sense at all."

I didn't have a feel for her sense, though I thought she was too distant from her kids. "You deduce that how?" I glanced at Charlie.

"That makes three days running with him."

I did not understand why everyone went "Ohh" in that rising and falling tone that says "major screw-up." It did not seem like a good time to mention who Kurt worked for, though it was probably Ulf himself who was the cause. He had been really chummy with Melanie on the lift. Three days with an ordinary instructor couldn't be the problem, could it? I hid my confusion in my beer mug.

Which is why I didn't see Egon walking up. My first clue that he was there was his heavy hand on my shoulder and his accented voice from behind, saying, "So, Hero. Out to celebrate with your friends?"

I wasn't going to turn around for him. "Shut up, Wuss." "Hero" was not any word I wanted new friends to attach to me. Julie and Mark glared at Egon—they'd let the subject go when I'd flinched during the introductions. I picked his hand off my shoulder and let it drop. "Get lost."

He laughed, and now I did turn around, intending to stand and run him off if a sitting glare didn't do it. My initial assessment, that he would be handsome if he could muster a pleasant expression to soften the heavy brows, high cheekbones, and formidable nose, was correct, except that he was laughing at me. "Oh? You do not wish to be hero? So sorry." He left to go stand near the darts players, and I heard him suggest to Dave that he'd play the winner.

"Hero?" Kim asked. When she cocked her head, it gave her the air of a poodle, with her alert brown eyes and mop of brown corkscrew curls. "Let's have the rest of the story, and no, you don't get another drink!" She glowered me back into my chair. "Not until you explain."

I really did need another escape hatch in a bar.

"Jake went up after Todd," Julie told her, and the rest of the group started to jabber. This had to be what Egon wanted, to make me uncomfortable. At least I'd be at the top of the lift tomorrow, not the base with him.

"Don't make a big deal out of it," I said, but the damage was done. Charlie had whipped out his cell phone and punched up a video. Damned Internet. The wilderness had no people and no cell phone towers. Friends were highly overrated.

The bastard passed the phone around, to the oohs and ahs of the group. Kurt came back to the table to stand behind me and have his turn to see what had happened. He let the video scroll out where we could both see it. I tried to watch through his eyes, but I was reliving the fear that Todd would plummet past my hands. He handed the phone back to Charlie and squeezed my shoulder hard. "You did good, Jake." Then he returned to his game like it was no big deal, but I was sure we'd have a talk tonight about my technique.

"You did," Mark said, and then he changed the subject, to my intense relief, asking Marty, a thirtyish man with wire glasses, shoulder length hair, and an academic air, about the snow conditions on the upper mountain. They were off and running on something that sounded too technical for my tastes about slabs and cornices and whether they'd need to assess some of the upper slopes for stability. Chelsea snuggled against

Marty's side and poked him when he expressed concern about depth hoar. Wasn't sure I'd heard that right, but I had other things to think about.

I tuned one eye back to the darts game behind me, answering Kim's question about where I'd learned to climb with one word and then asking the newbie question. "What's a cornice?"

"A place where the snow extends out over a void, like at the top of a hill or over a drop-off. The wind creates them. They're tempting but dangerous. They'll break off underneath you," she told me seriously, like she really needed to warn the novice to stay off the steep places.

Kurt had won the game, big surprise, and Dave was pulling some bills out of his pocket. "Here you go, sharper."

"I did say we should keep the stakes down, Dave." Kurt was having to deal with the consequences of beating the local champ, apparently. "How about I buy you a beer with the winnings?" I shook my head in wonder; it had been a while since I'd watched him work the legendary charm on new people. "Take your warm-ups, Egon. I'll be back in a moment." He and Dave headed to the bar, while Egon hurled his pointed weapons toward the dartboard.

Kurt came back to take a swig of his drink, which was disappearing as slowly as mine. He set the glass down and cautioned the beaming girls against finishing his beer, then went back to the darts alley where Egon was retrieving the darts.

"Friendly game? Or do you want to play for money?" Kurt asked Egon as he examined the fletching on his darts.

"Friendly, but with stakes." What Egon said next was too low for me to hear, but it changed Kurt's face, and not for the better. Egon went on. "A win for everyone, no?"

"No. Forget it." Kurt stuck his darts into the corner of the dart board and left Egon standing. "Not interested."

"Oh, you save it, then?" Egon grinned nastily at Kurt's back.

Kurt turned around and snarled, "Fuck you." That made everyone at the table who hadn't been tuned to this conversation swivel around and stare.

"You did not want?" His voice was mocking. I wanted to get up and pound his big nose until it stuck out the back of his head, but Kurt squared himself in that "one more comment and I'll punch you" way that made Egon back down. "Okay, okay." He strolled down the alley to the board to impale his darts, leaving Kurt furious.

Kurt sat down in the one empty chair with a crash and drained the rest of his beer in one angry gulp. His face was thunderous, and I thought he needed to get away from the group until he calmed down. I'd never seen him this mad—what the hell had Egon said? The bastard was back to say something else. He leaned over Kurt's shoulder and said clearly, "Good night, Alpenschlössl," before sauntering away.

That caused a little stir in the group; their eyes narrowed, and some of them repeated the name. What the hell was the problem? I wanted to ask, but I wanted to get Kurt out of there even more, before he exploded at everyone.

"Think it's time for us to head out of here, guys. See you again another time." I stood up and stuffed my arms into my coat. "Come on, Kurt."

He rose and grabbed his jacket without putting it on. "Good night, everyone, sorry to leave it on a note like this, but it's time to split. Better next time, okay?"

I added, "Good night, all." He headed to the door without

a backward glance, though Egon got a scowl across the room, and I was close behind him.

"Good night, Hero!" That made me flinch, but not nearly as hard as when someone behind me followed it with, "Good night, Zero!"

The cold night air was a bracing shock after the warmth of the pub. I caught up with Kurt halfway to the shuttle stop. He started ranting before I drew even. "So what! I work for Alpenschlössl! I teach them to ski! What the fuck is the matter with that?" He turned to me, eyes blazing. "Huh? What is the matter with that?"

"Nothing, Kurt." I spoke softly, trying to calm him.

"Then why…?" An unsuspecting snowman standing outside a restaurant took a swift uppercut to its frozen round head; snow exploded everywhere. "Why does everyone act like 'Alpenschlössl' is just like 'leper'? I teach skiing, damn it!"

"I know you do, Kurt. You're a good teacher. I don't know what's up with them. They're being idiots." I put my hand on his shoulder and hoped he wasn't so enraged he'd punch me just for attracting attention; the snowman had had a remarkably large carrot nose. "Come on, buddy, calm down, okay?" Getting tossed in jail for creating a public disturbance would be a rotten way to end the night. "Let's go home."

He fumed silently on the shuttle ride back to the apartment. He was a little calmer when we got off, and by the time we were back inside our little home, he was almost himself again. Maybe six months of almost no company except me had left him as intolerant of crowds as I was. Once inside, with jackets shed, he turned to me and held me tightly, silently. I held him as he clutched me, his head resting on my shoulder, facing away. We stayed like that until he finally said, "Come to bed with me."

I was tired and wrung out—bed sounded good. I'd find some energy if he wanted to make love, but he led me gently to the bedroom and left his shorts on when he slipped into our bed. I curled around him, holding him against my chest. He pulled my arm around like a blanket. I kissed the back of his neck softly, and I thought he was going to say something. He started to, once or twice, but sighed back into silence. I was almost asleep when he stroked my arm and said, "Jake, I... I'm glad you're here."

FIVE

Kurt was still subdued when he got up the next morning and got ready for work. I wanted to ask him just what Egon had said that had angered him so, but replaying that exchange in my mind, he'd probably offered to play for sex. It sure sounded that way. Other things about that were strange too, but that just might be Egon's English, which was good, fluent even, but didn't always contain the words you'd expect to hear. If he wasn't reminded about that, Kurt might just get back to his sunny self before meeting his client for the day.

We danced around each other quietly getting ready. He laid out clothing on the bed, which of course he'd made first—the man always made his bed, even if it was just snapping the sleeping bag straight, though his socks tended to migrate randomly. The ski pants were by a well-known designer, though they'd been purchased via online auction for a fraction of their cost at retail.

"I still don't see how ski pants could cost seven hundred dollars a pair, unless they came with Krugerands in the pockets.

Do they keep you six hundred fifty bucks warmer?" I tried to tease him.

"No, they keep you just warm enough." Kurt did smile at me as he pulled on silky underlayers and thin socks. This sort of clothing would help him blend in with the clients, a problem that I didn't have. He'd helped me choose winter gear online, though I had gone for good but less glitzy brands. Between us we'd spent a lot less than seven hundred bucks outfitting, though it helped that Kurt had some nice things from previous seasons. Now he pulled on a fleece shirt, the same one he'd worn to his interview.

Sitting down on the battered green couch that I'd rescued out of a charity pile on a sidewalk in Boulder, Kurt put his boots on and then came into the narrow galley kitchen where I was making some sandwiches. He threw some soup into the pot to heat while he located the lids to the thermos containers. No sense in paying resort prices for chow, even with the employee discount, though Kurt would have lunch with his clients twice this week as part of their ski package.

"I don't know who I'm booked with today, so I might be able to get by your station at lunch. We can get some runs in." I felt kind of bad when we did that, since it limited him to the bunny run and the green runs, which he told me were a little more challenging than what I'd been doing. I needed to pick up some skill with skiing, and fast, to keep Kurt from getting bored. It was hard, because I was still apprehensive about skiing again after so many years. When I was twelve, it had been two lessons and one broken ankle. "After your lesson last night, you should be rocking and rolling."

"I'd like that." Mostly because I was feeling weird about not being with him all day, every day. After six months of each other's constant company, you'd think I'd be ready for fresh faces and other people's conversations, but after last night, I remembered why I was so content to be alone with Kurt for days at a time. I poured the soup into the thermoses, threw the food into the insulated bags, and went to find my boots. The shuttle would be by in a few minutes to take us both to work.

There were a dozen different accents on the shuttle, as our fellow denizens of employee housing came to the resort proper, to clean hotel rooms or rent skis, maybe to wait tables. Many of the resort crew had the same sort of visa that Egon did, though I wondered how much intercultural interaction a hotel maid from Poland could really have with the wealthy people who came to the mountains to play. They took the jobs that were hard to fill with Americans, I knew, though Egon's job was one that ski bums competed for. It was odd that I got the job, since I had no skiing experience. What I'd really wanted to do was drive a snowcat, grooming the slopes. I could drive a medium duty truck, so I didn't think a snowcat would be a big deal.

Turned out that driving the snowcat was no big deal, and if that was all it took, they could have trained me to do the winching to keep the cat safe on the forty-degree slopes. No, it was the grooming, knowing when to pan, when to blade, that was the skilled part of the job, and they didn't want to train a neophyte on that here in BigBucksVille. Do a season at Eldora or Meadowlark and another at Breckenridge, and they'd consider letting me groom their frozen assets. Never heard of Meadowlark, I'd said. That was kind of the point, they suggested. But they'd liked my willingness to take on the task, so I got thrown what was considered in some circles to be a plum job.

Egon didn't think operating the lift was so plummy, I discovered that first day. He took out his frustration on the handiest target, me, though I was only trying to learn every-thing I could about my new job.

"*Shovel the snow off the wait line and the loading line. Pull the lever toward you to slow the lift, push it away to speed up. Do nothing fast. Complicated, no?*" *My lift partner had just taught me everything he considered necessary for me to know about my new job, other than* "*Call the ski patrol if something happens.*" *Okay, we were the grunts, there to get people seated in the chairlifts, not any kind of rescue team. Egon had made that abundantly clear in his accented sneer.*

We were on the bunny slope lift, which was fine with me. You could come down on one side of the lift or the other; there were no other options. Other lifts went higher up the mountain to the blue, green, and black slopes, but I'd have to learn the terrain first because I couldn't give anyone sensible advice yet about the slopes and their conditions.

There were a few early morning novices out, and long stretches where we just watched the chairs swivel around the pulley and come by empty. During one such lull, I stuck my head into the control hut where Egon sat.

"*What's all that stuff for?*" *I asked.*

"*The ski patrol uses that. You and I are not to touch it.*" *He sounded like Ah-nold, but he'd already rebuffed my questions about where he was from.*

"*I should know what the stuff is, at least.*" *Maybe logic would help. Curiosity didn't seem to be getting any answers. I had to get back out to the lift to seat a young woman with a little girl in tow, and then came back to ask again, once they were twenty feet away and had the safety bar down.*

"*That is the toboggan,*" *Egon deigned to inform me.* "*The stretcher, those should be obvious. The pulley, that is for rescue on the chairlift, if the chair cannot be reached from one of the towers. The patrol rides it down the cable from the next tower."*

Bending to look closer, I asked about something vaguely familiar. "This looks like rock climbing equipment." Rope and hardware lay coiled in the corner.

"It might be. Again, for rescues on the chairlift. Put that down," Egon instructed me with some annoyance. His dark brows were drawn up over deep brown, nearly black eyes, and his formidable nose made the scowl complete. He'd be handsome if he could look pleasant, but so far he'd glared, sneered, or scowled at me while I tried to learn what was what.

"It's a rock climbing harness and ascenders on a rope. I can't hurt it by looking at it."

"There are people waiting, go." Egon didn't quite snarl at me.

Just for contrast, I smiled widely at the skiers who were waiting to be seated and was rewarded with a nervous giggle from a preteen girl in a purple parka. "This is the bunny slope, right?"

"Yes, it is. Have fun!" I could be pleasant to these people who were here to have a good time. Egon could stay in the hut where no one had to deal with him.

That was a week ago. Last night he'd used the name of the ski school as a way to attack Kurt because he'd been so angry at not getting the job himself. I didn't understand this at all. Today, it would be a huge relief to be at the top of the hill, nowhere near him.

SIX

It might have been Egon's spiteful voice that had called Kurt "Zero" on our way out of the pub, though I couldn't be certain. Truth was, I couldn't be much angrier at him if he was the one, because the more I thought about it, the more certain I was that he'd wagered sex, and then set Kurt up for some humiliation when he got turned down. Though he might have wanted to set Kurt up for humiliation any way he could, just for getting the job. Asshat.

Such were my thoughts on the lift ride to the top of the bunny hill, my hiding place from the press. It might have been overreaction, but it really did seem like a good idea. Today, I'd watch the bunnies unload. At least I'd see any cameras coming up the hill. Wonder if Egon would make them buy lift tickets first. After last night's little nastiness, I didn't trust him not to let them on anyway.

It was snowing lightly, and it persisted all morning. Cynthia, the other lift attendant, and I took turns unloading and taking hut duty. She didn't complain about being out in the weather, though I wondered if her partner, Tom, was faring as well at the bottom or if Wuss was hogging the hut again. The thought of warm soup was pretty enticing, so when I caught the chair to ride down at lunch, I damned near walked into the camera crew.

I might have gotten away, though, if Egon hadn't pointed me out. "Ah, here is your hero," he sneered, and the perky reporter latched onto me harder than Todd had.

"I can't talk to you guys without clearing it with my boss first, honest. I can't." She kept begging and clutching, and I kept trying to get away without actually dumping her on her spandex-clad ass in the snow, which might have made some entertaining footage, albeit bad public relations. "Please, let go, miss." Maybe if I called her "ma'am" she'd get huffy and lose her grip. Tom, in the control hut, had thought fast enough to have gotten on the radio while Egon was out making trouble for me, because my boss was heading across the snow toward us.

Roy caught me at the base of the bunny lift, shaking my head and trying to get my arm back. "Miss, please let go of my lift operator," he said.

"This story will be so much better if Jake talks with us," the reporter said, brandishing the microphone with a Channel 9 logo attached. "Otherwise, it will just be that video that's all over the Internet. Please?" She flashed the sparkly whites that would get her hired in a heartbeat in a gift shop here in Wapiti Creek. I wondered how long it would be before Channels 4, 7, and 31 would be chasing me down too.

"What questions do you want to ask?" he wanted to know, and we negotiated carefully while the cameraman looked for the best background.

So, I spent my lunch hour explaining in very little detail about how Todd came to topple and about the rescue, showing distressing tendencies—I was sure it would get edited out—to talk about rock climbing, and mentioning Egon's role in making the climb possible. The wind was starting to whip up, blowing the needles of snow into Ms. Perky's unprotected face while I droned on from the warmth of my scarf. She'd get edited out, with that tendril of hair that kept flying across her face to make a lopsided mustache every time she turned to keep the slope and the lift in the background. She'd never make anchorwoman, I thought uncharitably, if she didn't have the sense to braid her hair for the slopes.

Channel 4 sent Ms. Businesslike, who had dressed sensibly and styled her hair for the wind, and a cameraman. They spotted us before Ms. Perky was finished with me. While waiting their turn, Roy laid out the ground rules, giving me hope that I might get to my hot soup before dark.

"Late again, I see," Ms. Perky told Ms. Businesslike with a smirk as she and her crewman headed out.

"He'll be more polished, now he's practiced with you," she shot back, and it was true, I sounded a great deal more succinct. Being cold and hungry had something to do with it too—I wanted to be finished and gone before any more cameras showed up.

"Please, let's do it one more time," Ms. Perky asked, but no, I could not wait to get away and was a little gruff saying so. Roy hadn't left, so he tossed his head toward the warming hut; they accepted the inevitable from him.

Except that it wasn't the end, because Julie and her little class had come to the bottom of the hill.

"Jake! Jake!" Todd and Gracie had to ski over and hug me; all the while Gracie was telling the fascinated reporters about how wonderful I was and why. The cameramen scrambled to point their equipment at this manna from heaven. Roy, horrified, stepped between us and the crews. I tried to hush them.

"Julie!" I bellowed, and she came skiing over to collect her escapees. She shepherded them away after I promised to wave at them from the lift every time they went by. "Don't you need me to sign a release or something?" I asked the reporters.

"There's no one around who can sign releases on the kids," Roy pointed out to the crestfallen reporters, and we stood around signing waivers while the class loaded up on the lift. Deprived of targets, they trudged off, and I made my escape soupward. Roy headed up to the lift, where I hoped he'd chew off large pieces of Egon's hide. As I strode across the snow, I glanced over at the retreating news crews and saw, to my horror, three cameras and three reporters, all chatting in a clump. Oh no. I think I ran the last hundred yards into the staff hut faster than I'd skied down the bunny slope yesterday.

"There's people out there looking for you." Mark swung into the chair opposite me.

I pulled the top off the thermos and inhaled the steam. "Rat me out and you'll be wearing a ski pole for a necklace," I said with a grimace. "I gave two interviews and that's two too many." The sandwich took the brunt of my ire as I ripped apart the bag.

"But you're photogenic and heroic and all that crap." Marty joined us with his lunch. The steam from his own thermos fogged his glasses—he took them off to let them clear and blinked at me.

"Crap is right. I can't wait for the furor to die down. Don't you dare give me away. Egon already fed me to the reporters once today." I took a swig of soup and felt the warmth trickle all the way down. I'd been standing in the cold for at least an hour with the reporters, not moving nearly enough to keep warm in the wind and blowing snow. Ms. Perky had to be feeling slightly ill. She'd been losing heat steadily off her head because she'd chosen stylish earmuffs instead of a proper hat, and if she was still prowling around outside, she'd pay for her fashion sense. I was dressed for conditions and was still glad for the curative properties of hot chicken soup.

"The wind's blowing from the northwest, been coming over the rise beyond the West Peak," Marty said, and that made Mark look at him sharply.

"How much deposit, could you tell?" he asked, his own food forgotten. Great, we were in for more scintillating conversation about— oh, yeah, I was interested in snow conditions, now that I was a ski bum. I'd ignored most of what they'd said at the pub, being more wrapped up in Kurt and the drama, but this might be good to know.

"The cornice over Cement Chute looks bigger, but there was so much blow I couldn't measure it." Marty took a sip of hot tea. "I think we should leave Cement Chute and that section blocked off until after we assess the next storm. That cornice triggers avalanches," he informed me.

"It's too damned bad we can't just leave that run closed, declare it off-piste, but it's way too tempting for the black diamond boys." Mark grimaced. "We'd be losing a few every winter if we didn't monitor the snow. One more good storm and we can trigger."

"How?" I'd seen movies of avalanches set off with rifles.

"One way, the accidental way, is to be standing on a cornice when it breaks off, but that tends to create openings on the snow conditions team. Mark and I prefer to use the howitzers. Little noises won't do it." Marty grinned at me. "If we can't start the slab moving by sawing off the cornice and bouncing it down the hill, we get out the big gun."

"Slab? I thought it was all loose snow rolling down the hill?"

"No, that's sluff. Not so dangerous. The slab is the top layer of snow that breaks free and slides—that disintegrates as it goes. It can get to eighty miles an hour pretty fast, which doesn't give the hotdoggers much time to get off the slab when it starts." Marty whooshed with his sandwich to demonstrate. "Been a lot of traffic to that cabin back of the cornice," he went on.

Mark gave me a strange look and went on eating. "That's off-piste."

"Sure. It's not on the resort proper even; the boundaries are just this side of it. The slides miss it, for which we should be grateful. Don't want to be digging anyone out. Post-slide snow is like concrete. If you don't get found in about fifteen minutes, you might not survive, and if we don't find you in two hours, we might as well leave the bodies there 'til spring." Marty sounded like he just didn't want the work, but I was thinking of what it might be like to get caught in an avalanche and how it would feel to die like that. Didn't seem much better than burning in a forest fire, a fate I'd already sidestepped once this calendar year. My appetite abandoned me for a few minutes, but I forced myself to finish the soup.

Then my appetite fled permanently, because out the window a cameraman and another man were stopping passers-by, asking them questions. Everyone they spoke to shrugged or shook their heads, but I felt like I had a great big target on my back, to go with the great big 7 on the camera.

"Oh, great. I have to get back to the lift, somehow. Can you guys distract them?" I must have sounded hunted, because Marty laughed.

"Tell you what, we can give them endless information on snow. Falling snow, powder snow, snow suitable for making margaritas…."

"They might care about sliding snow more," Mark

suggested. "We could use the exposure, maybe convince one dumb kid to stay out of a slide chute."

"Thanks, guys." I stuffed my lunch bag back into my locker and waited for the two ski patrollers to decoy my hunters away. They strolled past the camera team, stopped to answer, and then they were off and running, asking questions and motioning to the cameraman that he should start filming, pointing up at the slopes and making explanatory hand motions. They were just as photogenic as I and had much more interesting things to say, so I slipped out of the staff hut and pussyfooted back to the bunny lift.

"That was low, Wuss," I snarled at Egon from the loading line. "I better not see cameras coming up the lift."

He only laughed.

SEVEN

Kurt got off the shuttle opposite the Alpenschlössl office. He'd been so glad to get this job; he hadn't told Jake, but he had big plans for the money that he'd expected to earn over and above what he'd made last year. Jake had confided a dream to him back in the cave while they were waiting for death, and he wanted to make it come true for his partner.

Now, he thought as he crossed the street, dodging the big SUV that honked at him, this job looked like a big mistake. He hadn't mentioned the knowing smirks on the lift operators to Jake, nor a snide remark in the lift line, and Egon's suggestions last night had been just too much. Kurt was only sorry he'd punched the snowman and not that miserable bastard, who wasn't any more pleasant than Ulf. He didn't know how Jake put up with the guy all day long.

Highly recommended, that's what Rudi had said—he'd been recommended by someone who spoke very highly of his skills, and that was the only reason that Rudi was taking him over another candidate.

Of course, that was after he had gone back into the office

with Rudi. Jake was sitting there, waiting during the interview, and what Rudi wanted was bad enough, but to think that he wanted it while Jake was on the other side of the wall was just disgusting. Only the thought of getting his partner to Vanuatu with the big bucks made him go back and accept the position, sign the contract. Before he'd stomped out, the position Rudi told him to assume was on his knees, mouth open. No way. No way in hell. Kurt knew he was good enough to be hired at any of the other ski schools in town without any of this casting couch bullshit, and Rudi should know that Jake was his partner. Jake, who had said he was a happy man. Kurt hadn't wanted to tell Jake about this, knowing his partner would be unhappy about it, and besides, he'd turned the guy down firmly and still gotten the job, so no harm, no foul. Kurt smiled, thinking of Jake, so unsure of himself sometimes, but cast as the hero of the hour, and for good reason.

He was still smiling when he got into the office and headed for the equipment locker. "Hey, Amber, what's on the docket for today?" No garlic in last night's dinner meant he might even score one of the "*zur Burg*" packages. He smiled at the young blonde woman with the gamine face and hair and the thighs of a serious skier. She was cute, if you liked girls.

"I have Ulf out with Mrs. Underwood, again. She's economizing, apparently. She's got Ulf as a *zum Heim* this time. That girl is going to be ready for the Olympics, or something," Amber said, snickering. "Rudi's got one of his regulars flying in from California, and I, dear man, have been booked *zur Burg*."

"Good for you. Who's my student *du jour*?" Kurt hoped it was someone hardy, because the weather was crappy, snow and wind. He didn't feel like listening to endless whining.

"You are my student *du* moment, because I have just time

enough to show you the computer. Sit down." Amber motioned at the desk. "You're the booking agent today."

"I am?" Kurt stared at her. "I haven't the foggiest...."

"Sure you do. You teach them to ski. Here's the rate screen. Don't book anyone on a *zur Burg* unless they're on this list, but don't worry about it, if they haven't been offered it before, they won't know about it. This list," she said, clicking to a different screen, "is okay for a *zum Heim*. Don't offer that unless they ask, and everyone else gets *zum Berg*. Don't screw it up; there's a big difference in rates. Got it? *Zur Burg, zum Berg?*" Amber repeated, like he didn't get it the first time. "And don't book more than one *zur Burg* on any given day."

He'd picked up enough German in his years on the racing circuit to know the articles, if not always to use them correctly. "I got it," he said irritably, tugging at the neck of his fleece shirt. He hadn't dressed to be inside all day. Half of this stuff was going to have to come off.

"Here's the calendar, add the names in the slots and click 'save,' and you can surf on the net or whatever the rest of the time. The rest of us are going to be too busy to back you up, so I had to turn down that last client. She booked you for tomorrow, and she sounds thrilled about it, so you make her happy, okay? *Zum Heim* for her." Amber flashed him a big smile and pulled her hat on.

"What's different about that than what I've been teaching?" he asked, but he was talking to empty air, because Amber was outside greeting her client, an older man who chivalrously picked up her skis and offered her an arm. "Guess you'll tell me tomorrow," he finished glumly. "Great." He gave the phone a crusty look. Cursing the luck that had put him indoors turned to a smile when a gust blew a swirl of flakes past the window.

He hoped Ulf, that muscle-bound jerk, got plenty of snow down the back of his neck.

Layers of clothing got folded neatly on a chair, including the top layer of socks, which he'd picked up from their roost beneath the chair, thinking about the grief Jake gave him every time a stray turned up. Guess he had a point; Kurt's socks did appear in the strangest places. Comfortable now, he sat down to wait for the phone to ring, and in the meantime, he could update his blog. He'd been better about that lately, since they didn't have to wait until the weekly trip into town from the rangers' cabin. He'd updated from the Meeker library all summer, but he had Internet at home for the first time since last spring. He had a lot of good things at home now—home was where Jake came back every night.

Wonder if Jake had looked through that contract yet? He'd been concerned that Kurt had signed it without reading it thoroughly, but really, Colorado was an "at will" state; it wasn't as if he couldn't leave if he wanted to, or that Rudi couldn't really fire him if he was so inclined. Kurt peeked through the file drawers, looking for a blank that he could read more thoroughly since he had all this time while the phone wasn't ringing.

The phone stayed stubbornly silent during his hunt, but what he wanted was probably in Rudi's office, and that door was locked. He shook the door handle, wondering if he could pick it, but it looked too solid for his burglary skills, which were limited to simple locks he could unlatch with a credit card. Jake would be shocked to discover there was something he couldn't do. Kurt was a little embarrassed about how his lover thought he could do anything, sometimes, but the things he couldn't do well didn't often come up in conversation. Aside from backing big trucks down steep roads.

He sat down, preparing to browse the web for something

entertaining. Maybe find the real difference between the *zum* and the *zur* and why a mountain would be referred to both ways. If he got bored enough.

Business! He picked up the chirping phone, all set to be professional. "Alpenschlössl Ski School, this is Kurt…."

Keeping his face straight while he quoted rates was the hardest part of the call, but he gamely made the prices sound extremely reasonable, extolling the virtues of the mountain, the skill of the instructors, and the great strides in skiing the clients could hope to make. By the end of the third such call, Kurt thought he'd done well to book two of the three callers to lessons, credit cards and all. Then the phone stopped ringing, and he had time to get bored again.

Kurt had just watched, for the third time, the dramatic footage of Jake's rescue in all its gritty, grainy glory on a video site. This one was destined to be a classic of its kind. Had the news crews come up from Denver yet? Honestly, Jake just didn't give himself credit for how fast he learned things, nor how well he applied them. Kurt shook his head slightly and decided to find his lunch, made by Jake's caring hands. He thought about all the things Jake could do with his hands. *Keep up this line of thought, old man, and you're going to have to whack off.* Would serve him right, too, after what he'd put Jake through last summer.

While munching the sandwich, he'd started flipping idly through the client lists, just to see how many names he recognized. Yeah, there, and there, and that one sounded familiar…. He leaned forward, forgetting to chew, when he spotted a name that he knew. Damn, he hadn't seen that one in a while. Not since he'd left from that very address on the climbing trip to Yosemite that had ended his friendship with the man's son. Benji.

He still grieved that friendship, two and a half years later, though so much had passed since then. He didn't remember Mr. Shaffer as much of a skier, though. Wonder what he was doing on the *zum Heim* list. Kurt swallowed hard and pulled up the client history: a couple of lessons, one with Rudi, one with a man who no longer worked with Alpenschlössl. Something booked for January, again with Rudi.

Putting his thoughts aside as idle curiosity, Kurt finished his lunch and tried not to think about how much that climbing trip had changed his life. It had shaped some of his life's decisions, bringing him to his lover, and eventually the two of them to this ski town in the deep mountains.

The phone rang, the fourth time since he'd been trapped in this office. "Alpenschlössl Ski School, this is Kurt. How can I help you?"

The voice on the other end was warm and cultured, making him think of pearls and silver teapots. "Hello, dear, I need to book a ski lesson, for one, intermediate. Who's teaching this year?"

Oh good, questions he could answer without a hard sell. "Rudi, Ulf, Amber, and me. I'm Kurt; I'm new here this year."

She laughed, warm and throaty. "New, oh good. I adore new instructors—they so often have new techniques to teach. Or something to learn. Tell me, dear Kurt, are you open the week of December sixteenth?"

He clicked through to the calendar. "Yes, ma'am, I'm available from the seventeenth on." It was comforting to have bookings so far out, he thought, because he felt a little more secure than with straight walk-in traffic for private ski lessons. Having a booking turned away this morning made him nervous, though he was salaried, not on commission.

"Perfect. You'll be a little early Christmas present to myself, then. Put me down for the seventeenth and the eighteenth. *Zur Burg*. I want this to be a very nice present to myself; I deserve it." She purred, making Kurt warm from his teaching being considered a very nice gift, though he'd never had anyone but Jake sound quite that enthusiastic about it before. She was on the list and booked a couple of lessons every year.

He took her name, which he had seen in financial magazines, and her credit card information, before she asked, "How will I recognize you, dear boy?"

"I'm five ten, blond and blue eyes, with a dimple. And an Alpenschlössl pin on a red parka." Good grief, was he supposed to send pictures? Post his face on the website? Did they have a website?

"Ah, yes, that pin does convey quality, doesn't it?" She laughed deep in her throat. "So, how long is your gear, dear?"

"Huh? I mean, I use parabolic one seventies for teaching." He'd never had a student ask that.

"Never mind, Rudi only hires the best. Ta, ta, dear. See you in December." She hung up, leaving Kurt staring at the phone, dead in his hand.

What was that all about? He'd been booking a ski lesson, and she'd behaved as if she'd purchased a great deal more than instruction. Why did the length of his skis matter?

The client clearly knew the difference between *zur Burg* and *zum Berg;* Kurt rattled the words into the search window and discovered he knew a lot less German than he'd thought.

Everything Rudi'd said during the interview took on a second, more sinister meaning now. Had he missed every double entendre in his innocence? Had Rudi's demand for some head been a sincere part of his interview? He thought back to what he'd said and despaired to know that he had said things that could be taken every bit as ambiguously. Rudi had asked Jake if he was all right with this job, managing to get a reference on Kurt's prowess at the same time.

No, Jake would not be all right with this job, if it was what Kurt suspected it really was. He was not all right with this job, if he was expected to do more than teach. The way their new friends met every mention of his ski school last night meant he'd missed a critical difference between two similar-sounding words.

This was unreal. He couldn't possibly have stumbled into what he feared, although the high salary and the problem with garlic breath niggled at him. Kurt put his hands over his eyes and rubbed, turning these horrible developments over and over in his mind. This couldn't be right. But just in case his worst fears were true, he was going to protect himself.

You'd think he'd learn to come right out and ask the questions he needed answers to. He'd danced around the important things with Jake for far too long, and he hadn't questioned things about this job when he should have, blinded by the money. He'd ask Rudi tomorrow. And he'd take a good long look at that contract tonight; he needed to know what he'd agreed to, and if he could get out of it. He'd been too quick to assume that the contract would only protect him.

In the meantime, he started copying lists, posting them into his blog as unpublished posts, because he could think of no better secure location for the files. He could be wrong, but if he wasn't, he'd never get another chance to get into the files unimpeded.

He had to be wrong. He just had to be wrong, but Kurt had a grim feeling that this time he'd figured it all out too late to do any good.

EIGHT

The weather cleared as the day went on, leaving the Colorado sky that unbelievable blue streaked with clouds, though another storm was forecast. Improving conditions lured more skiers out, and I even saw Mrs. Underwood and Ulf doing a run with Todd and Gracie, who'd been out since early morning. What kind of mother did that to her children? In better weather, I'd understand it, but I thought this morning's weather was too rugged for little kids, though Julie had had two others beside these. Either Colorado kids were tough little guys or mom and dad weren't going to let anything spoil their vacation.

No more news crews found me, and I hoped that no more would seek me after the two stations aired their interviews. Then I could stop skulking around, though it would mean going back down with Egon, who needed a good punch in the snoot. I debated clobbering him before, or after, he explained exactly what the deal about Alpenschlössl was, because obviously neither Kurt nor I understood it.

Kurt was pensive when I got home, distracted. He barely

reacted when I told him about being stalked by cameras, though he did turn on the television to catch the news. Silent when I suggested I'd make dinner, he excused himself to take a shower, while I wondered what was going on. If it was left over from last night, it was hanging on a long time. Kurt didn't usually prolong his brooding.

He came back out in sweat pants and a T-shirt, hair wet and curling at the ends, face still glum. "Jake," he said, "I think I've made a horrible mistake."

"Come here, Kurt," I said, patting the couch next to me. "We'll figure it out."

He sat, but not close enough to me for my liking. I tried to pull him closer, but he sat like a stone. "You might not want to cuddle me after you hear."

"That's bull. Get over here." I got one hand hooked around his shoulder and pulled him against me, where he finally softened enough to put his arm over my stomach. "So, tell me."

"It's the job. It's why everyone snickers. I'm an idiot."

"If you are, you're my idiot." I kissed the top of his head. I wasn't worried about him being an idiot; he was the most capable guy I knew.

"Maybe not for long," he mumbled into my chest, making me squeeze more tightly.

"Now, that really is bull. You are mine." I wanted to say "I love you," but I didn't want it to mean "don't be upset."

"Jake, you might not want me after finding out how stupid I've been."

What? "Kurt, that is the first truly stupid thing you've said. I want you." He resisted at first when I tried to tip his head up for a kiss, but relented and let me find his mouth. Crushing his lips to mine at first, then softening to gentle nibbles made me realize how much I wanted him. He kissed me back with desperation—his vulnerability aroused me, and the gentle nibbles turned again into fierceness. "I want you."

"I hope you always do, but Jake, this is important." He wasn't letting me pull him over on top of me, which brought my mind a little bit away from sex.

"You were right. I should have read that contract carefully. It's going to be a bitch to get out of," he said miserably.

"A bad business decision isn't going to change my mind," I said.

"And I should have asked why the pay was so much higher than the market."

"Because it's all private lessons, and you're the best." I tried to kiss him again, but he moved. I had to shift my erection inside my jeans—I was still aroused and listening was hard.

"It's private all right. My student that first day had a *zum Berg* package, that's 'to the mountain.' But there are two other levels. I've been grumpy about not getting those clients, but it's a good thing I didn't." He sat up and put his elbows on his knees, looking at the floor before he looked at me. "Jake, the *zum Heim* package I think means the instructor goes to the client's condo or hotel. It means 'to the home.' And the *zur Burg*, it's 'to the castle' and we can only book one a day, and it costs twice as much as the *zum Berg*. I should have twigged sooner, but I learned my German on the fly and didn't figure out it wasn't all 'mountain' until it slapped me in the face."

I thought of the cabin back of the cornice that Mark and Marty had mentioned. "A lot of traffic lately," they'd said, and the knowing looks they'd exchanged suddenly made sense. A flash of Kurt and a client skiing out to the cabin twisted my gut with jealousy. My imagination made the client someone older and richer than me, and put a purchased smile on Kurt's face. "I think I know where the castle is, and you aren't going out there with anyone. You're mine!" I yanked him savagely into my arms and sought his mouth fiercely. "Mine!" I said into the kiss, then pushed my tongue against his.

His arms were like steel bands around my chest, bands that should never be released. "I don't want to, you know that. So I'm quitting, right now." He kissed me back just as hard. "But I've been stupid."

"You're my stupid!" His T-shirt ripped as I hauled it off him. "Mine! Idiot or not!" Oh, he was an idiot, but we'd get him out of this somehow. How exactly was going to have to wait, because I was so frantic at the thought of other people touching him, paying to touch him. I couldn't think of more than touching him myself, covering him, leaving no bit of skin unprotected.

My T-shirt went, and then I flipped Kurt to his back on the couch, the better to haul his sweats down off his ass, his beautiful ass that no one else could touch. Grabbing his rounded cheeks would keep other hands away. I'd be there first, I thought wildly, as I bit and licked the inside of his thigh. Maybe a bit too hard, in my frenzy—he yelped but then lifted his leg so I could reach better, and this time he moaned as I swooped around his hips, grabbing hard to hold him near.

"Mine!" He couldn't think that I'd reject him for making a bad decision—I'd make love to him strongly enough to convince him. He had to know I wouldn't turn him away for this. My jeans came down—I could barely stand to take my hands away from him long enough for stripping, but I was naked now and threw myself on top of him. He was warm and welcoming. Once again his arms were tight around my chest, and he shifted his hips under me. His erection pressed against my own. Good! I would touch him there, no one else, he wanted me there as badly as I wanted to feel him, and my mouth was savage on his. "You're mine!" I gritted into his ear, turning him enough to lick the edge of the shell, knowing he loved that and that no one should do it but me.

I had to touch all of him, every part. My touch would protect him, shield him, arouse him. He started to kiss me back, up and down my neck, with the fierceness of teeth behind the kisses, devouring me as I devoured him: ears, neck, shoulders. We struggled to mouth each other as I lay over him.

Suddenly I needed to feel the reality of Kurt with my hands. I slid to my knees beside the couch, though I lay over his chest, mouth never stopping. I used a hand to touch his hard cock— I'd stroke him, pleasure him, and strike away any other hands that dared reach. He was throbbing against my palm—the little veins pulsed against my fingertips when I measured his arousal with fingers and thumb, knowing this was for me. "Mine," I growled again, stroking slowly, firmly, possessively.

Kurt groaned his pleasure under my mouth, but so frenzied was my need that I couldn't do one thing for long. I stroked him and then had to cup his balls, being careful not to crush, but needing to feel how he responded to my touch. He clutched me tightly, mouth to mine, tongue dancing against mine. From his balls, I had to slide my hand behind his thigh, gripping the strong muscles, feeling their play under the skin, and then back to his ass, gripping one cheek and then sliding into his crack with the flat of my hand.

"Mine!"

I had his thigh again, for leverage to pull myself away from his mouth, his warm mouth that I couldn't leave unguarded while I traveled down the hard planes of his chest and stomach. So I slipped a finger between his lips, feeling how he swirled warmth as he sucked. I cried out before I reached his cock, having marked his skin with my saliva, and now I took him in my mouth, where none but he could go. Hard and thick, throbbing, his cock filled my mouth as I worked over him, trying to take in his every inch, though seven usually defeated me. T

Tonight I was wild, desperate, and saying "mine" once again opened my throat to engulf him to the base. I needed him safe within me, and I could take him to the base. It was enough that he was wet to the hilt. I let his cock slide out and then licked the head around for claiming. Again he filled my mouth, stopping my words by thrusting to meet my tongue, entering me for joy if not refuge, and he was marked by the wetness of my mouth.

I wanted to fuck him. I was between his legs in a flash, ready to penetrate his ass, but frenzy seized me again. I hadn't claimed enough of him with my mouth, nor had Kurt had anywhere near enough preparation to cope with my cock. "Mine!" I insisted, as I came down again to kiss him, to plaster my whole body against his, to bite gently against his neck, and then I was on my knees again, his heels on my shoulders, and it wasn't enough.

I lifted his hips with a tug to raise his ass into the air and let his knees come down against his shoulders, letting me see, touch, and lick all that he had. His face was a wonder as I pulled his balls into my mouth one at a time, but still I could do nothing for long.

My tongue traveled across the plane of his taint to the crevasse only I could explore. "Mine!" I roared, and plunged my face there to slide my tongue across his hole, claiming him for mine, mine. This was new, this claiming. I'd wondered about it but never ventured—now, Kurt's ass was mine, mapped with saliva and traced with tongue. I held his waist tightly, lapping him, stroking him, making him understand that he was taken—mine.

He cried out for my touches, but now his moans were full-throated and guttural. Nearly upside down as he was, he sagged against my chest, and only my arms around his hips kept him balanced on his shoulders, letting me devote full attention to exploring him, learning his ridges and opening. He blossomed under my tongue—the tight muscle relaxed with my probing and licking. This I would do for a long time, to make him ready to accept what we both knew could hurt him if I was careless.

I would not be careless with this man who was mine; I would pleasure him, treasure him, protect him, even from myself. I'd hesitated to fuck him when we were new together, because I wasn't sure my thick eight inches would fit, but he'd shown me how, and we never hesitated again. Now, I would prepare him with licks and kisses to take me inside.

My frantic need to see his face made me lift my head. He raised his hands to me, and I pulled him upright to crush him to my chest before taking his face in both hands to look deeply into his eyes. Did he understand that he was mine, that nothing he'd done could change that? I gazed into Kurt's blue eyes, heavy lidded with the pleasure I'd given him, and he smiled. His dimple showed he understood, so with fierce tenderness I kissed that dimple, flicking my tongue briefly into the sweet hollow that only showed when he was happy.

I pulled him to my chest again before want made me push him backward. His hard cock needed reclaiming—I knelt again to bob my head over his groin, taking his cock into my mouth as deeply as I could, not as deeply as before, but deeply, repeatedly, enough to make him moan. I tasted his salty, musky skin as long as I could before the greater need took me.

He had to be wet again—I needed to make my final claim upon him. Kurt helped me flip his butt toward my face once more showing me his sweet ass slicked with my spit but needing more. "Mine," I reminded him, before swirling my tongue across his tender pucker, poking the wet where he'd need it in seconds.

Kurt needed it now, because I'd let his butt down again and was ready to push inside him. The head of my cock, so hard it damned near hurt, touched the wet at his ass, before I shifted my hips in my only careful move of the night. This first joining took all my care, and then I could only buck against him, thrusting into his hot ass with strokes that grew longer, harder, and wilder. Bracing one foot on the floor let me stay upright, to look down into his face as I fucked him, to see how his face reflected his pleasure at being taken.

Kurt's lips were parted as he panted; his gaze on my face as I thrust. "Mine!" I said again, feeling the climax building, threatening to sweep me away. Unstoppable as an avalanche, my orgasm pulsed through me, rolling down into Kurt, who dug his hands harder into the cushions. I slammed into him one last time.

"Mine," I whispered now. My hand closed over Kurt's cock —he'd spend himself only for me. I knew how to touch him. I'd learned what he liked and gave it to him now as I clasped him, stroked him, claimed him. My cock was still inside him as I rolled soft skin over hard shaft, bringing him closer to climax with every move. He went over the edge, thick white come spurting from him as he called my name, the only word he'd said since I'd first claimed him as my own.

Exhausted, physically and emotionally, I lay down against

him again, not caring about the spatters. Kurt held me against his chest, his lips to my hair and his hands softly stroking my back, returning me to rationality.

"Mine," I muttered, my heart aching that he'd said nothing so far.

I could feel his lips moving with the one word that could comfort me. "Yours."

NINE

We woke the next morning clutched in each other's arms, having barely moved from how we'd fallen asleep. The bed was one of the best things about a town life. Sleeping entwined hadn't been possible in our camp cots, and the deer mice that inevitably found their way into the cabin had chewed holes in the air mattress faster than we could patch them. If we snuggled, it was outside on the ground, usually near the lake. The lake was frozen over by now, but the bed, with the new burgundy striped sheets, slept on by nobody but us, was warm and comfortable.

We'd come back to bed for another round of sex last night after treating ourselves to a celebratory meal. Rudi had no more say over what Kurt did or didn't eat. Defiantly, we'd gone out and devoured a garlic chicken pizza with extra sauce, and if he'd answered the phone, Kurt could have told him so. Take that, all would-be *zur Burg* clients!

I moved my head just enough to be able to kiss the tip of Kurt's nose. One blue eye opened to look up at me, making me smile. "Good morning."

"Good morning to you." He rolled to his back, pulling me against his side. "It's going to be a better morning in just a bit, because I'm going to call Rudi and tell him I quit."

I'd looked at the contract finally and was worried about that. "Did you look at the severance clause?"

"What about it? He can't make me prostitute myself, Jake. Contract or no, that's illegal."

"Yeah, but that contract doesn't specify what exactly your 'duties' are, and he can sue for 'expected revenues for the remainder of the season'." I had thought about that before falling asleep. "The rates for the base lesson times the number of days you'd reasonably teach is more than double what you'd make teaching at a regular school. There's got to be a way out that doesn't cripple us financially for a couple of years."

"You said 'us.' Jake, this isn't your problem." His hand was warm on my arm.

"After I convince you you're not an idiot, you say something idiotic like that. Your problems *are* my problems." I wove a leg between his. "But I don't see this going to court. Besides, can you just imagine how that would sound?" I used a sonorous, pompous tone for the lawyer's voice, and my own for Kurt's words:

"'*Mr. Carlson, before you attempted to quit, had you been instructed to do anything other than teach skiing?'*

'No, but I'd figured out that I would, soon.'

'Based on what evidence?'

'The word on the mountain was that the school was a front, and the clients were too friendly.'

'Oh really? Based on rumors and a few fluttering eyelashes, you are attempting to deprive Rudolph Gernsbach of revenues he could expect from the legitimate operations of a ski school.'

Then the judge says, 'pay up'. Nope, that won't work. Even if it might take a while to play out."

"I don't see it going to court either, not the least because I'm judgment-proof. What can they take away from me? Some sporting equipment? My biggest asset isn't something they can turn into cash." He kissed my forehead softly.

"No, but if Rudi thinks that your biggest asset is that ass you're setting on, do you really believe he'll try to keep you to the contract by legal means? This whole thing is outside the law to begin with."

"Well, now, that is true, and what's the worst thing he can get?" Kurt chuckled wickedly. "Too much publicity, that's what. Ask me what I stole yesterday."

I sat up abruptly. "Kurt, what did you steal yesterday?"

He laced his fingers behind his head and grinned. "I have the entire client base for every sort of 'lesson' sold in the last three years, plus this season's bookings, parked in a nice safe place, where he'll never find them. Lots of recognizable names."

"Whoa, that will twist his tail, but even if you make it public, he'll just say, 'these fine people ski better now than they did before they came to us, and that is all'." I had to admire the beauty of the set up: hiding right in plain sight.

"But will these fine people ever return to Alpenschlössl? The ski'n'sex packages aren't offered to just anyone. Amber told me that." He looked puzzled for a moment. "I guess there has to be a referral system, or no one would ever book *zum Heim* or *zur Burg* to start with."

I lay back beside him, leaning on one elbow. "That would cut the heart out of his future earnings, for sure. For that matter, Kurt, why did Rudi hire you? Why did he think you'd go along with this?"

"I don't know, Jake. Everything he said could be taken two

ways, and I didn't make it better with some of my answers, because he ticked me off, and I got kind of smart-mouthed." He looked chagrined.

"Great. What did you say?" Kurt could say some outrageous things.

"He asked if I gave good head, and I shot back that I gave better Salomon, like we were talking about brands of equipment. It seemed witty at the time, and he liked it, but I thought he just figured I'd entertain the students."

"That's exactly what he thought, Kurt."

"Yeah." He pulled his mouth to one side, thinking. "He did make it plain that he expected some, but I thought it was one of those 'make the sap compete for the job' things an asshole boss would do, because there'd be some who'd do it, just to get hired. I told him no and made it stick, and you saw what happened next—you were there."

I remembered. "Yeah, the happy man probably convinced him you were good at it and willing."

Kurt lifted up to kiss me. "I am willing, but only for my happy man. We'll both be happier once I tell Rudi I'm quitting."

I rolled on top of him, clutching him tightly. I would be a lot happier once he was free of the ski school.

He broke off the kiss with, "Crap! I'm booked for a lesson today! I've got to get down there and head it off! Jake, I know it's your day off. Where are you going to be? I'll find you, and we'll have a great day together, okay?" He rolled me off him and was into the shower.

"You could just teach it, earn the bucks, if it's a regular lesson." I stuck my head into the bathroom to talk to him and ogle him in the shower as a bonus. The man was gorgeous, covered with soapsuds.

"It's not. Amber said *zum Heim*, and I'm not going to her hotel or whatever." My heart leaped to hear that.

"Do you want me to go with you?" I slipped into the shower with him, a tight fit, but rubbing against him was the nicest way to get clean.

"I should be good alone. What I do want you to do is get into my unpublished blog posts and look at the names, see what you think. It isn't like anybody's being mistreated, and Rudi sure didn't pick Ulf, Amber, or me up at the bus station to exploit. I'll leave you the password." One last kiss and he was out of the shower for a quick stop at the sink, where it was a miracle he didn't slice his chin off. I reached for the shampoo and was still in the shower when he poked his head back in to say a quick good-bye.

It was all going to get better. Kurt could find another job quickly, and if he couldn't, well, we didn't have to stay in Wapiti Creek. Anywhere would be good with me.

I lathered up, thinking back to last night—I'd been so desperate, and he'd been so pliable. "Yours," he'd declared himself to me, and we'd been so intimate. Condoms were a fact of our sex life, but we hadn't used them last night, and I'd never licked him between the cheeks before. He'd done it only once, briefly, to me. I'd made him stop, afraid I'd disgust him, but I hadn't even thought about that as I'd tongued him, wild to claim him.

Considering that made my cock stand up, begging to be stroked. Touching myself and thinking about Kurt was nothing new, just nothing I'd had to do lately. Before the big fire, I'd jacked off two and three times a day, yearning for him, not knowing he yearned for me. Now I only had to reach for him. Waiting until he got back wasn't an option. I remembered too well how he looked lying on the couch with one leg wrapped around me and the other foot resting on my shoulder, hands dug into the cushions. Remembering how it felt to have my cock buried in his ass, I stroked myself until I came, spurting come the way I'd spurted into him last night. I had to shake myself before I could turn off the water and find a towel.

The password wasn't strong enough. I laughed and switched the caps around until it read "I8jaKe" instead, which I scribbled under his old password. Then I stopped laughing as I read the names on the lists. Some were recognizable names—political, financial, and entertainment—but others I had to search the web for, and I gulped. More power probably rested with those people, and not a one would appreciate having their name associated with scandal. Rudi might fight harder to protect himself than I thought. Retribution could come from other quarters. We'd have to do something to defend ourselves.

Kurt's blogging software had a delay feature on it. Posts could be published on prearranged dates. He had a post set up, written two days ago, set to publish on Thanksgiving, that made me warm inside as he talked about finding someone, though he spoke in general terms. Thinking about that, I checked his stats. Enough people followed his adventures as a skier, ranger, and outdoorsman that this news could spread fairly fast.

If he published the lists of the *zur Burg* and *zum Heim* clients, word would get around. The number of followers made me whistle and revise my estimate of how fast Alpenschlössl would hit the major news arteries—a lot of people read his words. Rudi needed to do the reasonable thing and turn his unwilling employee loose. I hoped for everyone's sake that Rudi would do just that.

The phone rang.

"Hey, Jake, I have good news and bad news." That twisted me up inside. "The good news is that my client decided that she dared not have a *zum Heim* lesson since her husband decided to get up here a day earlier than planned, so I have a pair of students who will do a two-hour lesson of nothing but skiing, and any screwing around this afternoon will be strictly between them."

"That doesn't sound like the good news we wanted, though. You're still teaching for Alpenschlössl." I sat down on the green couch where Kurt had lain last night.

"That's the bad news. I can't find Rudi. He's out with a client, and his phone is turned off. Amber just looked at me like I was ripping up lottery tickets, and Ulf, well, I'm not going to discuss it with him." That sounded like a bad idea all the way around. "Why don't you and I go skiing before I have to meet the Walkers?"

"Sounds good!" The few runs we'd gotten in on my lunch hours only whetted my appetite for more. Of course, the "ski lesson" I'd gotten in the kitchen had the same effect.

"I'll be right home." I could hear the smile in his voice as he promised. It matched the one on my face.

TEN

The snow was incredible, groomed to a perfection that I now recognized as skill. The storm had dropped another fourteen inches over what we'd gotten earlier in the week, making base out of what the snowcats had packed down during the storm and leaving the last few inches that fell as powder.

My abilities were sufficient to deal with top powder, but not more. If Kurt wanted to play in the champagne powder that lay two feet deep in the upper bowls, he'd have to do it alone or with another partner. Mark, Marty, or Kim could have joined him, I suppose, but I'd already waved at Kim, who was patrolling down the blue slope adjacent to the chairlift, alert to trouble. After the storm, I supposed Mark and Marty were doing tests and whatever else they did with fresh snow.

"Come on, Jake, time for some green slopes," Kurt said, inviting me to follow him to a different chairlift. "You did everything perfectly on the bunny slope, you're getting used to the feeling of speed, and it's time to stretch a little. Let's go up the mountain a little higher."

I was feeling a lot more confident now. Three runs on the

bunny slope and only one fall: I was shifting my weight on the skis exactly the way Kurt had coached me in the kitchen. That teaching technique would be a big hit with the Alpenschlössl clientele, though they'd never get to benefit from it. Every time we'd gotten back to the lift line, Kurt had tried calling Rudi again, leaving messages that started as "I need to talk to you" and ratcheted up to "I won't be back tomorrow."

I wouldn't have to get on the lift under Egon's supervision, either. He'd made a big point of slowing the lift for us to load, like we did for the smallest skiers, until I growled at him. Then he'd inquired if I was getting my money's worth, nodding at Kurt, who still had the school pin on his red parka. On the last trip up the lift, I managed to clip Egon's shin with my ski, suggesting he wuss out back to the control hut before any little kids hurt him.

"Egon Bachov, sounds familiar," Kurt mused halfway up the hill after that last altercation. "There was a Bachov on the Bulgarian ski team for a while in the nineties who did fairly well on the World Cup circuit, but this guy's too young. Might be family."

"Might be a common name too," I said, wondering why Kurt would know obscure stats from so long ago.

"Maybe," Kurt agreed, with a faraway look. "Have to check. Anyway, unload to the left and then do shallow turns until we hit the base." Once there, he'd directed me without discussion to another lift that would take us to different terrain.

This was more like skiing as I'd imagined it. The first trail we tried wasn't much steeper than the bunny slope, and the scenery was better. A wide swath between the evergreens made the feeling of mountain more complete. I got all the way down without a hitch, earning the same kind of approval that I'd gotten for my first bulls-eye on the archery range. "That deserves a kiss," Kurt said softly as we skied toward the lift line. "Payable tonight."

"The interest rate is exorbitant on kisses left for hours," I replied, equally softly, though we weren't near the lift lines yet. "Might involve taking your clothes off."

"Do this next run well, and I might have to take your clothes off to place it." Then Kurt laughed as I fell over trying to stop.

Oh, there was going to be some wild kissing tonight. Kurt had taken me down a different easy run that had a steep pitch in it that probably could have earned the run a blue designation if it wasn't easy to avoid, which I didn't. I took that run on the steepest possible angle, though I did lapse into a snowplow once. "Good!" he cheered me. I'd gotten to the bottom without falling. "Let's do one more green run, and then I know a blue one you should try."

This was the most relaxed and happy I'd been since we'd come to Wapiti Creek. Basking in Kurt's approval, doing something that was getting to be more fun and less hard work, knowing that our worries were going away, all served to make me next thing to giddy. After that third green run, I was ready to kiss him right there in front of the world when someone called his name.

"Carlson? Kurt Carlson? Is that really you?" A big, thirtyish man swung up in a spray of snow, a huge grin splitting his face. By big, I mean he stood at least two inches taller than my six feet and had to outweigh me by twenty pounds, maybe a lot more if he was as solid as he looked. He was fit, muscular, and he'd managed to sweep Kurt nearly off his feet in a bear hug.

"Hey, Jorey! Put me down already!" Kurt thumped the newcomer's back.

"Glad to! What the hell did you eat?" Jorey let go of Kurt

just before the steam started coming out of my ears. The garlic chicken pizza was worth every cent.

"Hug repellent, but hey, it's good to see you! What are you doing here?" Kurt seemed genuinely glad to see this guy once he was free.

"The team's following the snow around, and they won't let us train at Beaver Creek—there's a race there in a couple weeks. Wapiti Creek has some good slopes for training, you know? A couple of runs are a lot like the Val d'Isère. Remember that?" He grinned as Kurt shook himself back into shape. "I ditched the team on the East Peak."

"That's just you all over." Kurt turned to me with answers at last. "Jake, meet my old pal, Jorey Taylor." Kurt introduced me to someone whom I'd only seen in magazines and on the television, flying down mountains faster than anyone else.

"So, Kurt, what are you doing here? Come into some bucks?" He grinned. "You're looking good."

"It's all that fresh air. I'm teaching here." Kurt grinned back, but there was an element of strain there.

"Awright! Is he good?" he asked me, eyes dancing.

"The best," I replied firmly. The guy might be a legend walking, but I didn't like the way he was making Kurt uncomfortable.

They chatted, catching up with each other as Kurt loosened up. He seemed genuinely glad to hear of his old friend's successes, letting him do most of the talking. They sounded like they knew each other from way back, making me wonder what else I didn't know about Kurt. It wasn't that he was secretive; it was just that he lived so much in the moment that a past was almost hard to imagine.

"So, you guys headed up to the West Peak?" Jorey asked, and Kurt shook his head. "Damn, I thought we could come down Dynamite Alley. It's a lot like the course at Alta. Remember that?"

"How could I forget?" Kurt asked wryly. "It was the first opportunity Jorey had to kick my butt down a mountain," he explained to me. "He was thorough."

They'd competed? I took another look at my lover, seeing a part of his life I hadn't shared, couldn't hope to share.

"It was the first time we'd raced in the same class," Jorey added. "You did some butt kicking too. I just kicked a few more of them."

"Always do. Always have. Unless you smear your own butt across the mountain. Finished any more downhills on one ski lately?" Kurt teased him, apparently not bearing any rancor for the defeat.

"Nah. Never did get that other ski back," Jorey reminisced. "So, maybe change your mind and do Dynamite Alley with me? Both of you?" He turned to me, forcing me to admit that I had no business on that piste at all.

"I'm not up to the black diamonds yet." Probably I'd never get an invitation to ski with an Olympic champion again, but damned if I was going to ask him to do an intermediate run instead.

"That's for next week. Give him a break, Jake just started skiing," Kurt said easily.

Jorey turned to me. "Hey, I'm not cutting into lesson time, am I? Because I really want to take Kurt down that hill, like old times."

"It's fine with me," I told Kurt. "I'll watch if the run is visible from somewhere I can get to."

"If you come down Sugar Gulch, to about even with Tower Three, you can see Dynamite Alley. In fact, you can be the starter and the judge. Get off at the top of the Lower Scott, and we'll take the next lift up while you're doing Sugar Gulch," Kurt told me. "We should end up at the top about the right time."

"You're going to race?" I asked, knowing that one of them had been skiing the bunny slope with me while the other had been training for World Cup events.

"Of course." Kurt elbowed his competition. "It's what we do."

ELEVEN

On the quad chairlift up, Jorey bombarded Kurt with questions about his life since leaving the ski team. I listened quietly. No surprises there, though Jorey couldn't seem to believe that Kurt was really content with a life that didn't include racing.

"No kidding, you were a ranger the last couple of summers? What did you do for excitement?"

"It was plenty exciting—you have no idea." Kurt winked at me. "Death defying experiences come in more forms than eighty miles per hour down a mountain."

"Don't tell me you gave up your unicycle riding? What about the trampoline?" Jorey rattled on.

"Didn't drag any of that up to the mountains. I do a lot of archery and rock climbing, and skiing is more fun now than when it was a job." Kurt was starting to sound a bit uncomfortable again. "Jorey, I don't miss the endless training."

"You can't say I didn't come up with fun ways to train, Kurt. Better than the coach's ways." I began to suspect another round of new skills for Jake coming up, just from the way Jorey rattled Kurt's cage about the past.

"The unicycle cost me a shot at the Olympics, Jorey." Kurt explained to me, "We did it for balance training, but I came off one of those parking barriers and twisted an ankle before a qualifying race, so I had a sore ankle and a sore ass. The coach chewed my butt for what seemed like days."

That didn't sound like "better" to me.

"Archery, Kurt? Archery? Where's the glory there?" Jorey wanted to know.

"I could kill you silently at fifty yards."

I was beginning to wish he would.

"Remind me not to irritate you, man."

Too late. I was a pretty good shot now, come to think of it....

"I can still cuss you out in six languages, Jorey."

Now that sounded like a skill he'd need to teach me.

We unloaded at the top of the Lower Scott lift. Kurt waved me on to Sugar Gulch, which was marked blue. I lifted an eyebrow and got a smile and a wink in return. Okay, I'd do it.

"We'll wave at you when we're ready, Jake. Both arms down to start us, and you're the finish line too. See you in a few minutes." Kurt and Jorey headed to the line at the Upper Scott, which was Gabe's lift. I hadn't seen him since the other night, but I could go days without seeing the other lift attendants.

Sugar Gulch was fun—I allowed myself to pick up more speed. The turns weren't different, though I discovered I could shed just enough speed by turning frequently, if shallowly. One edge of my ski caught on something, which sent me tumbling, but I picked myself up and kept going, unseen by anyone other than a pair of teenage boys on snowboards, who hit the snow themselves not much farther down. It was almost too soon when I reached the wide spot where the runs converged.

I looked up the steepest run, figuring that was Dynamite Alley, and in a few minutes tiny figures at the top waved at me, Kurt in red and Jorey in blue and white. Setting my skis into a reverse snowplow so I didn't skid backward down the hill, I held both arms above my head. They crouched in a start position; I dropped my arms abruptly, and they began their hurtling descent.

I kept forgetting to breathe, watching them throw themselves down the mountain. Kurt stayed near Jorey as they turned only enough to stay on the fall line. If my efforts could have sped him, Kurt would have passed Jorey—I urged him onward with each heartbeat. Still, the gap between them widened as they came toward me at impossible speeds.

I counted seconds after Jorey blew past me, marking one chimpanzee, two chimpanzee, until four primates had been totted off and Kurt sailed by. I turned to watch him stop, just in time to see Jorey grab him again, thumping his back and laughing.

"See, man, you still got it! Why ain't you still racing?" Kurt looked small, crushed against the big guy's chest, and not happy to be there.

"I still have it, just that I don't have the desire for it, Jorey." Kurt smacked the side of his fist against the racer's arm. "Let go, already." His voice was muffled because half of his face was smashed into Jorey's parka.

"Okay, but man, you made me work for that." Jorey calmed down and let go.

"You still ski like a cat thrown across an icy driveway," Kurt told Jorey, a wry grin on his face now that he wasn't being clutched.

"A cat that's been thrown real fast, Kurt. Hey, I'm supposed to catch up with the rest of the team. Gotta go, but I'll tell everybody I saw you, okay?" Jorey pulled back his sleeve to look at his watch and turned to ski away.

"Yeah, and good luck in Beaver Creek and Kvitfjell." Kurt wished him well. One side of his mouth quirked. "So, want to go do Sugar Gulch again, or do you want to try Sundance?" He turned to me. "It's the intermediate slope I mentioned."

"Is it harder than Sugar Gulch?" I refused to drag Kurt any farther down from his ability level than I had to.

"About the same. It's fun."

"Let's do it." I was ready to try to match Jorey's breakneck journey down the mountain.

On the chairlift ride up the hill, I asked, "When did you race?"

"Jake, it was a long time ago. It's done." He tipped his head back and closed his eyes.

"But you were only about four seconds behind Jorey." He'd looked so fast as he'd come down Dynamite Alley.

"Jake, listen carefully, okay?" He took his sunglasses off to look me full on now. "I have always been four seconds behind Jorey. Four seconds is what separates first place from last place in a World Cup race. Sometimes six seconds, if it's a really long course, which Dynamite Alley is not. I didn't make the Olympic team on my one and only shot. I wasn't on the American team ever again after that. There were too many guys that were just that tiny bit better. I'm good, I know that, but I'm just not quite that good." He looked straight ahead again after he stopped talking, and his eyes glittered, which might have been from the wind. He put the glasses back on, but I'd seen. "The skiing paid for college, and it keeps me fed in the winter, but I'm not going to race at that level again."

"But...." I'd just seen him chase a champion down the hill,

untrained, and stay in range. What could he do if he worked at it?

"Jake, you saw one old friend beating, but not humiliating, another. Do you really think he was skiing full out?"

I shrugged. "Looked like it to me. He said so. He has a reputation for never holding back." I'd read the article at the Alpenschlössl office just a few days ago.

"He does. And for a couple of years, my nickname was 'Jorey's Shadow.' Trust me, he wasn't going as fast as he could. I was. I never finished higher than twenty-third. You can look it up. He just keeps getting better." Kurt's voice grew smaller with each word.

"You're number one with me, Kurt." I lay my hand on his thigh, mindful that we had only two more towers to reach the top of the lift.

"Thanks, Jake." He gave me a small smile as he put his hand over mine. "I... I like the life I have with you."

At the top of Sundance, Kurt stopped to warn me. "We aren't racing here. Take it easy."

This run looked steeper than Sugar Gulch, at least the part I could see before it curved away into the trees. Still, I wanted to take it at a level that would be at least entertaining for Kurt. Jorey had reminded him of glories past, but I needed to keep him happy in the now. Even so, there was a question that burned in my mind that I couldn't leave any longer.

"You said they called you 'Jorey's Shadow.'" He nodded. "Were you and Jorey...?"

Kurt wrinkled his brows, trying to find the rest of my sentence, and then he laughed. "Oh, hell no. He likes the girls. And I—" He pulled me over for a kiss, and he didn't even look around first. "—like you."

I fell three times coming down Sundance, and it didn't matter.

TWELVE

"You're doing great, Jake," Kurt told me. We swung past the lift line at the Lower Scott quad chair. "I need to head down to the bunny lift to meet the Walkers. I hope they ski at more or less the same level. It's an easier lesson that way. See you at home!"

We headed down a green run toward the bunny slope without turning to shed speed. I'd been working on trusting myself to stay upright as I picked up velocity. I could see why both Kurt and Jorey enjoyed the racing—this was fun! I planned to ski on my own for a while longer and then go find some lunch.

Of course, once I was at the bottom of the bunny lift, I had to watch Kurt ski over to a couple of strangers, one of whom had planned to screw him. I gave her a sour look and him a grateful one, for coming up early and interfering with her plans. Kurt greeted his students, suggesting that they do a bunny run so he could see their turns. I decided to start from the top of the bunny hill. Then I could get back over to the quad chair and make another couple of runs down Sundance.

That was before my girlfriend spotted me.

"Jakejakejake!" squealed Gracie, running the words together in her excitement. "This is my daddy! We're skiing together!" The five-year-old girl bounced up and down as she pulled into the roped off corridor for the lift line behind me. Daddy Underwood was right behind her, a tall, imposing figure craggy and gray enough to be her grandfather instead. Mama Melanie and Todd followed in his wake, though Todd pushed past to high-five me.

"Understand I owe you a debt of gratitude, young man," Mr. Underwood said, holding out his hand.

"Glad to do it, sir," I replied. "No debt." I had to take my hand back to pry his daughter off my waist. "Let go, Gracie." I'd been manhandled less by amorous adults whose intentions were direct and immediate.

"Let go, Gracie," echoed Melanie, who didn't seem so imperious in her husband's company.

"Jake should come skiing with us!" Gracie suggested, and Todd echoed her, tugging at my jacket.

"I'm sure Jake has other plans, children," Melanie said with a horror that I hadn't earned. We all shuffled a few ski lengths toward the loading zone.

I did have other plans, but Gracie yanked at my hand.

"Please?" she begged. "You're skiing anyway, right?"

"It is my day off," I admitted.

"Actually, Jake, I'd appreciate it if you'd escort the kids while my wife and I hit the higher slopes. I'd like to see what all these ski lessons have done for her form," Mr. Underwood said with an air of certainty that I would agree.

I did know who he was—he was the man who signed my paycheck. "Okay. What time would you like them back?" There went my afternoon.

"You're back on the clock until four thirty, then," he said

kindly, taking a little of the sting out of it. "And we'll arrange for some comp time tomorrow. Will that suit you?" We'd trudged up to the loading zone, which allowed Egon to over- hear it. He glowered at me, though he said nothing as Gracie and I slid to the loading zone.

Gracie told me everything about her day with Daddy, relieving me of the need to say anything at all, though I thought about how disappointed he might be in Melanie's newly acquired skills. Maybe Ulf had taken the precaution of teaching her something in the upright and clothed position.

I had the germ of an idea at the top of the hill—there was another way to pry Kurt out of Rudi's clutches. Surely James Underwood wouldn't countenance Alpenschlössl's less savory operations if he knew.

He was arguing with Melanie as they came up the hill. "Hon, he's passed the background checks." I hadn't known about that. "He's reliable, and the kids like him. They'll be fine." She started to protest further, but the chair dropped the three of them at the unloading station, where Cynthia did a double take at three in a chair. The boss makes his own rules.

"Hold up, kids." Todd and his father swung out of the chair, both skiing expertly toward us. "Jake, you three will want lunch, and the kids should have some hot chocolate midafter- noon. This—" He pulled a card out of his pocket. "—will let them put your food on my tab. You guys have a good time." He turned toward his wife, who was waiting at the side, looking very unhappy. "Oh, and Todd?" He turned back for a moment. "No black diamonds."

Great, he had just told a five-year-old to stay off the expert runs.

"Not even with the blue squares?" Todd wheedled.

"Not even. You too, Gracie." He smiled. "By the end of the

season, maybe, but not today. Have fun!" The Underwoods swung down the hill, leaving me with two kids. How exactly had that happened again?

"Where first, guys?" I'd done okay with Kurt, so I was not about to let five-year-olds, not even the sort who had to be warned off the expert slopes, outski me.

"Over that way, and we are going to ski all the runs that have a *B* in the name," Gracie announced. "I know how to write *B*'s."

"Okay, all the greens and blues that have a *B*." They started down the hill, and I watched the kids go hell for leather down the slope. Long skis go faster—I caught up.

"But 'Black' has a *B*," Todd tried to convince me in the lift line. The kids had come down the bunny slope using parallel turns, not the snowplow turns Julie had been teaching.

"Black has a diamond too. Dad said no." I found myself calling him Dad like he was my own father.

Todd looked mischievous. "He won't know if you don't tell him."

"I'll know." I used my best parental look, which probably was a total flop. "We do greens and blues." Maybe not—Todd just nodded acquiescence.

On the way up the hill on the quad chair, I asked about the turns.

"Oh, we did pizza turns when we were little. I don't know why Miss Julie made us do those, except that the other kids didn't know anything at all about skiing." Gracie was snuggled up to me. "You don't do pizza turns, either."

Well, no. Kurt had coached me out of those earlier in the week. In the kitchen. Melanie must have plopped the kids in any old class available, just so she could run off with Ulf. I felt sorry for them.

The kids and I chased each other down four runs with a *B*. By the time four thirty rolled around, we'd cleared the *M*'s as well, and we'd had a blast. My turns got faster and more accurate; my speed was probably twice what it had been that morning, and I'd fallen only once since lunch.

I felt damned near ready to take on Jorey Taylor myself.

THIRTEEN

It was a helluva comedown to go from chasing an old teammate with a chest full of Olympic and World Cup medals down a racing slope to coaxing a novice into using a proper parallel turn instead of the obsolete stem Christie turn he'd been doing since before the instructor had been born. Kurt pushed the thought away and encouraged Mr. Walker to keep his feet parallel and to bend his knees.

Mrs. Walker didn't need encouragement. She was acting almost as if the arrival of her husband hadn't spiked her plans for a *zum Heim* lesson. As if Kurt wanted to touch her under any circumstances. Horrible old bag with her eyebrows in the "plastic surgery/surprised" position and scrawny legs where she must have been over-liposuctioned; no way. Vanuatu would have to wait for a winning lottery ticket. Jake would appreciate that a whole lot more than he'd appreciate getting there on Alpenschlössl paychecks.

Of course, looking at Mr. Walker, Kurt understood why Mrs. Walker would fork over the bucktaters to get her mitts on him. He shivered, but not from the cold. Both students had many layers of clothes on, for which Kurt was intensely grateful. He'd also figured out fast to load the quad chair so that Mr. Walker was in the middle, after one ride where the old bat had slipped her hand under his butt about halfway up the hill. Her husband's attention was all over the mountain, which she considered a prime opportunity for groping Kurt.

"Look over there, Mr. Walker!" He'd pointed out a half dozen figures in blue and white parkas working on technique through slalom gates. "That's the U.S. Ski team; they're getting ready for the World Cup race in Norway next week." With his arm in front of the man and attention diverted, Kurt had been able to yank her hand out from under him, using a painfully tight grip on her forearm. At least, he hoped it was painful—too many layers of clothing might have saved her from his anger.

"Where in Norway, Kurt?" she'd gasped once he let go. "Zumheim?"

"They don't race in Zumheim any more, ma'am," he'd told her with a steely glare. He did not appreciate the reminder that she had originally booked him with the expectations of sex. "They'll be in Kvitfjell."

"When did they stop racing in Zumheim?" Mr. Walker asked, as if he had a clue.

"Back in 1995," Kurt said nastily, and made sure she had no further opportunities to grope him. Taking them down blue runs at the limits of their skills was his revenge. Mrs. Walker had to concentrate on what she was doing or risk going ass over teakettle. Kurt bade them wait and watch while he demonstrated the technique again and came to a halt a hundred yards downslope to watch the mess they'd make trying to reach him.

To his great surprise, Jake came pounding by with the hounds of hell after him. No, those were really small children—

they just skied like the hounds of hell. They were definitely after him: he'd pulled up at a fork in the trail, and they'd stopped to confer. What the hell?

"Wait up, Jake!" Kurt yelled downhill, and then, "Meet me at the fork!" uphill, and he took off in a skating start to reach the trio below. The Walkers would probably revert to turning with stem Christies from anxiety over being left for a quarter mile, but he'd sort them out.

That was twice today at race pace. Kurt pulled up just downhill from Jake and the kids. They were starting to ski away to the right as he got there and said "Hey!" No doubt because Jake hadn't heard him from so far away.

He'd never get tired of the welcome in his lover's face, he thought, as Jake stopped again and said "Hey, Kurt, where did you come from?"

"You have to pay attention to the other skiers, Jake. You blew by me up there. You looked great." Jake's smile got even wider. "Teaching the small fry how to do it?"

Jake laughed. "I'm trying to stay one step ahead of them. Kurt, meet Gracie and Todd. We met on the ski lift the other day." The man had a real talent for understatement, Kurt thought, and he demonstrated it once again by saying, "Kids, this is Kurt. He's my best friend."

That was enough for the kids to know.

"Does that mean you're going to leave us and go ski with him?" Gracie asked, twisting her mittened hands together. Todd's eyes grew huge at the suggestion.

"No, it means I want you to know who he is. We're going to ski together until your mom and dad meet us at four thirty, just like we planned." Jake's voice was gentle, and Kurt remembered how irritated Jake had been with their mother and her tendency to take off. How he'd come to be the children's escort was a story to be told at dinner. Kurt could hardly wait to hear it.

Gracie grabbed the tails of Jake's parka, and Todd lost the worried look. "Good. Kurt, are you going to come ski with all of us?" the little boy asked.

"It would be fun," he said, "but I have people that I'm teaching and they should be along right about—" He glanced uphill, noticed that Mrs. Walker was heaving herself to her feet as Mr. Walker stood by, and changed his mind about saying "now." "—well, in a minute."

"That's too bad. You'd take us on the black diamonds. Jake won't." Todd looked disappointed. "But he'd do it for his best friend."

Bet Jake hadn't mentioned the best reason of all for staying off the expert slopes.

"Todd, your dad said no black diamonds, and Kurt wouldn't get you in trouble with your dad any more than I would." Jake was stern.

"What makes you think I'd take you on black diamonds?" Kurt asked. An Underwood kid would almost have to be fearless on the slopes that were his birthright, but Kurt hadn't started the black diamond hills until he was seven.

"Because we saw you racing Jorey! You guys raced down Dynamite Alley! Jake," wheedled the girl, "Dynamite Alley has an *M* in it, and we're doing *M*'s now."

"No, Gracie." Kurt himself wouldn't ask Jake again after getting turned down in that tone of voice, but the kid was persistent.

"Jorey would take us! He's coming to dinner at our house tonight! We'll ask him!"

"Yeah!" piped up Todd. "Jorey's way cool! Or Ted or Nick!"

Good grief, was the entire men's team coming to dinner?

There had been other dinners in other days where Kurt, Jorey, and Ted had been the VIP guests. "Even Jorey has to ask your dad first, and I think they're all leaving for Norway tomorrow, anyway." Kurt was a bit stung at being classed as less cool than Jorey by a kid who probably couldn't speak three word sentences yet when Jorey earned his last Olympic medal. The arrival of the Walkers came as a relief.

"Later, Jake. Bye, kids." Kurt turned to his clients. They had about another fifteen minutes of his time. Just because Jake was tied up until four thirty didn't mean the Walkers were getting one extra minute from him.

"Later, Kurt. Okay, guys, let's go!"

Kurt asked his students to do two turns and then stop, but kept one eye on the disappearing skiers. "And go to the left, that's the green slope. I see we need to practice the parallel turns a bit more." Honestly, Jake was the best student he'd ever had.

Fifteen minutes later, Kurt shook hands with his students and suffered through a cheek kiss from Mrs. Walker. With assurances that the time had been well spent and enjoyable, claims that might have been equally false from all three parties, they parted ways, not one minute too soon for Kurt. Free at last, he got in the bunny line to use the hill to speed him over to the Scott lifts, rather than do a long uphill trudge. He had plans.

Jake, of course, wasn't manning the lift, but Egon was, discussing with a young woman whose turn it was to go to lunch. As Kurt loaded with a seat partner he'd acquired by yelling, "Single!" Egon had leaned over to speak into his ear, a looming presence in black and yellow.

"I know who you are, Alpenschlössl."

"You don't know shit," Kurt turned to snarl. "I'm not Alpenschlössl." The chair yanked him out of speaking range before he'd finished the words, while the teenaged girl next to him looked fearful. Kurt felt compelled to tell his seat partner that she hadn't really been trapped for a seven-minute ride next to a madman. She still headed to the other side of the slope when they offloaded.

Lift lines were mercifully short on this early season day, though not short enough to ride single in a quad chair. Kurt caught the Lower Scott lift to get halfway up the mountain, and then went directly to the Upper Scott, not sparing another glance for the big black and yellow signs warning the unwary that the Upper Scott served expert terrain only. He would have called Rudi again, but he didn't need the random strangers with him to overhear what he had to say.

"Hey, Kurt!" Gabe, whom he'd met the other night at McTavish's, called to him from the top of the upper lift. "Where are you headed?" He stepped away from the top of the lift to greet Kurt, who decided to stick around in the hope of a friendly word.

"What's good up here besides Dynamite Alley?" Might as well get it from a guy who'd know. Kurt hadn't been on the upper mountain but once.

"It's all diamonds or double diamonds off this lift, except for Killy's Knees, that's a blue, except they call it blue/black because of some good moguls at the bottom. Sec." Gabe darted at an oncoming chair to yank a young man's jacket free of the chair where it had fouled and threatened to drag the skier. He sent the man off with a wave and came back to Kurt. "Cement Chute is good, but it's off-piste right now, because of the avalanche danger, so try Hotdog Bun, or Say Your Prayers if you don't mind ending up at the Wildflower lifts. They're all good." Gabe grinned. "But I'm going to do Dynamite Alley on my way to lunch."

"Pretty good recommendation." Kurt had been planning to do that one again anyway.

"I'd go with you, but I still have half an hour." Gabe scrutinized a chair full of laughing teenagers offloading awkwardly. "Maybe later." He headed over to the small group, calling out, "Guys, which way are you headed?"

Kurt left Gabe to do his job. The patrollers should be grateful to a lift operator who kept the inept off slopes they weren't equipped to handle. These boys would probably end up on Killy's Knees, judging from Gabe's arm motions. Kurt swung around to find his way back to Dynamite Alley. Kurt didn't see the tall skier in the yellow and black parka offload, nor would he have expected to—he'd left the man at the base of the bunny lift.

FOURTEEN

Weather was moving in again. The blue sky was half obscured by the gray storm front that was forecast to drop another twelve to fifteen inches of snow. It didn't matter, though, since visibility was still good for racing. Blue shadows identified the terrain marks on the slope, letting Kurt see clearly defined features. He picked out the fall line and prepared to challenge the mountain.

Jake had been a distant speck at the bottom of the hill this morning when Kurt and his old friend and rival started from the top of Dynamite Alley, but now no one waited below. Only two other skiers showed on the slope now, one moving easily about halfway down, and the other almost at the bottom. He wouldn't endanger anyone while he recaptured his past.

Damn Jorey for patronizing him! They'd been friends once, and Kurt, for all that he'd been truthful about them not being lovers, had wished for it then. Most of all, though, they'd been competitors at the highest levels of skiing. He'd been "Jorey's Shadow" not just for their friendship, but for the way he'd trailed the bigger man down the hill. Sometimes he'd been a second and a half behind, sometimes two seconds, sometimes four, but always behind.

Kurt knew he'd done damned well for being a light man in a sport where weight mattered. He didn't bulk up hugely; he was a wiry 165 pounds competing for medals that got hung around the necks of men who outweighed him by thirty pounds, like Hermann Maier, or closer to fifty pounds, like Jorey. Gravity only had to love these guys enough to shave a few thousandths of a second off their times, and there was just more of them for gravity to love. There was a time when he would have traded what Jake called the nicest ass on the planet for a broad beam like Jorey's if it would have just gotten him down the mountain faster.

But not today. He was going to ski the hell out of this mountain with his own natural attributes, then he was going to plant his nice ass in bed with Jake tonight, and it would be the best of everything. He bent his knees, took a deep breath and a better grip on his poles.

"Reliving the races?" The scornful voice with the Eastern European accent coming from behind startled him.

"Fuck you!" Kurt had had entirely too much of Egon the other night—to have him interrupt now was intolerable.

"Here and now?" he mocked, letting his poles dangle from the wrist straps as he reached to his fly.

"Are all Bulgarians such assholes, or is it just you?" Kurt ground out. He'd just take off down the mountain, but the run would be spoiled anyhow.

"Are all Americans such fools, or only you?" Egon took his hands from his crotch. "To get such opportunities and waste them?" He regripped his poles and planted the spikes into the snow.

"What are you talking about?" Kurt demanded.

"Oh, you have good job, which you do not like, though it would bring you pleasure as well as salary. You could have been champion, but you played with foolish toys and called it training. Oh yes." Egon curled his lip. "I heard stories at Olympic Village. Jorey's Shadow hurt himself and Jorey took medals. I was there. I listened to Austrian and Norway national songs, watched flags go up."

"You were there." Kurt thought he knew everyone on the circuit. He'd tried to forget the talk that he knew had circulated among the elites of his sport, and now this unknown claimed that he was in on the secret.

"I, like you, did not finish on the podium, though I, unlike you, competed," Egon sneered.

"The last Bachov I knew about on the World Cup circuit retired years before. I think you're lying." Kurt hadn't had a chance to look the name up.

"No, that was my cousin Evgeny. He taught me to ski, though he did not suggest such stupid training methods as unicycles. I was not on Bulgarian team until last minute. There was opening when Gavril Dimitrov was injured." Egon looked grimly satisfied.

"I remember Gavril. He was real good on the giant slalom. What happened to him?" Kurt hadn't known the skier well, not having any common language, but they'd been nodding acquaintances on the racing circuit.

"Do you know what happens to seventh fastest man on team that can afford six in international competition?" Egon looked down that formidable nose at Kurt, making him aware that here was another man taller and heavier than he. "Is like what happens to eleventh fastest man when teams can have ten." Kurt knew only too well what happened to that man; it had happened to him. Egon's hands tightened on his poles. "In poor country that subsidizes athletes heavily, family no longer eats so well or heats home enough in winter." *How exactly had Gavril been injured?*

Egon didn't answer that question, but he answered "why." "The difference between lift operator's pay and Alpenschlössl instructor's pay matters to that man's family." Egon tensed, which made Kurt tense and then throw himself down the slope as the big Bulgarian lunged.

It wasn't the start he'd wanted for what might well be a race for his life—he'd been turned slightly and his path crossed Egon's. He felt the other man's ski pass over the tails of his, which could have spilled him down the slope, possibly providing the injury that Egon wanted, possibly providing paraplegia—or worse—on this forty degree incline. Kurt used his poles to shove himself faster. No time to explain he didn't want the damned job he'd accidentally taken away. A sharp pain in his side marked Egon's determination to hurt him. The bastard had stabbed him with a pole!

The wind in Kurt's face cut like windblown ash as he pelted down the slope. He'd raced against Jorey this morning, but the stakes had only been pride, not his life or spine. Any fall he took now would have devastating results even if he lived through it. Knowing that he was racing for such a prize made him sharper and somehow more alive. The mountain hummed through his senses as his skis slid over the snow. He carved through one of a tiny handful of turns in his breakneck flight to a more populated area. The trees were a green-black blur at the periphery of his vision. Crouched in a tuck with poles pointing back, he hid from the wind that would detain him.

To turn his head enough to see his pursuer would throw his balance off too much. At this speed, Kurt could well provide himself the career-ending injury Egon sought. Eyes forward, he hurtled down the mountain toward the runs' convergence. Any passing skiers were going to have to depend on luck and Kurt's quick reflexes. Fortunately no one blundered out into the junction.

One more turn and he was in sight of the lift. The crowd was his protection now—if Egon ran him down with witnesses, he still wouldn't get what he wanted. He'd have no lift ticket. Reckless skiers did not get to keep season passes.

Kurt pulled up at the lift line in a rooster tail of snow, heart pounding. He'd be very aware of his new rival, and rivalry it was, now that he knew Egon had participated in what he'd yearned for. He counted one Mississippi, two Mississippi until the other man appeared, which took six long seconds before he even came around the bend, enough time that Kurt could investigate his side where the ski pole had struck him and determine that it was nothing worse than bruising.

Egon skied past the lift line, studiously not acknowledging his lost quarry in any way. He did turn and flip the bird when Kurt shouted after him, "I always beat Gavril too!"

FIFTEEN

Danger past, Kurt got in line for another trip up the hill. He'd keep an eye out for Egon from now on. He wouldn't let the man tumble him into harm, though if he was on the black diamonds and the other man on the bunny hill, danger didn't exactly lurk.

So, he'd have a great time pelting down one of the other expert runs, though it might not be quite the same without something important on the line. Didn't matter—his blood was singing through his veins and the wind was giving him chilly kisses. The sun was out, for now, and it was all good. Except Rudi had again failed to pick up his phone. Kurt grimaced at the phone and shoved it back into his pocket.

Two lifts later he waved at Gabe. "Gonna try Hotdog Bun this time." Kurt turned that way once he offloaded.

"You sure? I'm about to leave for lunch," Gabe offered, making Kurt pause.

"Okay, I'll wait!" Kurt swung around, biting the snow with his edges. The competition was more important than the novelty.

Gabe grabbed his skis and stepped into the bindings. "How fast do you want to take it?" he asked as they ran the access trail.

"How fast can you go?" Kurt grinned at the man. He wanted something to add the spice that fear had given his last run, though without the danger over and above the run itself.

"Try to keep up!" Gabe pushed his poles into the snow to launch down the mountain.

Try, hah! Kurt followed, skating down the incline onto the slope proper. Gabe was setting a good pace, though he was turning more than a racer would. There was a twenty yard gap between them, closing fast, as Kurt rose to the challenge, taking a straighter line down the slope than his opponent. Damn, this was good! A dare, a mountain, and a beautiful day.

The pace was much less than his last two runs down this hill, but so were the stakes. Kurt drew steadily closer until he was nearly abreast of Gabe, who would probably take this next section as a straightaway. Kurt pushed off and tucked, shooting past Gabe and then sliding a little more through the next turn than he would have liked, but shedding some speed. This wasn't Grenoble, and Gabe didn't deserve a thrashing.

Down in the junction a little clump of skiers was heading out of Sugar Gulch. Kurt swung wide to avoid them and screeched to a halt. Gabe was a few seconds behind; he, too, pulled up.

"Guess you can keep up," Gabe panted, leaning on his poles.

"I try," Kurt said, instead of doing a victory dance. "We ought to do that on Hotdog Bun."

"Only if you like to slalom; there are gates all the way down for two abreast. Not my favorite." Gabe looked around for any oncoming skiers and then started toward the huts.

"Not without a full helmet and some shin guards." Kurt had

gone over too many gates to risk getting whacked in tender places. He followed Gabe toward the hut, but decided that he'd get one more run in before chasing down some lunch. Maybe he could meet up with Jake and the rug rats. "Catch you again sometime, okay?" he called to Gabe.

"Pass me again sometime, you mean?" He laughed and waved, skiing straight past the Lower Scott lift line.

Kurt swung in through the rope lanes, scanning ahead for his lover, but recognizing no one. His phone tweeted from his pocket—maybe Rudi was responding at last. Kurt shuffled forward a few ski lengths and groped for the phone. "Yes?"

"Kurt, it's Rudi. Where are you?"

"In the lift line at the Lower Scott. Rudi—" Kurt started, but didn't get to finish. Rudi talked right over him.

"Meet me at the bottom of the Upper Scott, then." Then Rudi was gone, leaving Kurt steaming. He tried calling back, but was treated once again to the "Ride of the Valkyries" ring tone, followed by an invitation to leave a message. He did, pungent enough to cause heads to turn ahead of him in the lift line, and then he thrust the phone back into his pocket with a scowl. Trudging through the lift line, he thought of all the things he was going to say to Rudi when he caught the man at last. "I quit," for starts, and then he'd find out just why Rudi had thought him willing to screw for pay.

The answer for that might result in an assault charge, he considered on the silent ride up the lower lift with strangers, because the more he thought about that, the madder Kurt got. He'd always chosen his lovers with care, the few he'd ever taken. Jake had never asked him about his past love life, though there might have been a lot of assumptions about it, especially since they'd always used condoms. Until last night.

A thrill ran through him at the thought of last night. Jake

had been so possessive at even the thought of him being with other people. Kurt didn't think it was just chest-thumping. No, he hoped it wasn't—he wanted a nice long future with Jake. He'd hoped for a future with Brad and again with Drew, and he'd known it was doomed with Rusty almost from the beginning, though he'd hoped against hope and kept trying long after he'd been left behind.

Only Benji had been a one-night stand, and even that had been born of hope. They'd been climbing in Yosemite when the weather had turned on them. Benji had clung to Kurt only as long as they'd clung to the side of El Capitan in the days of rain, wind, and lightning, and had offered something Kurt had never expected to get from his "straight" roommate and rock-climbing companion. He'd taken the comfort Kurt had offered, had initiated and responded to the kisses and the caresses they could manage on the narrow ledge, clipped to the rock wall with climbing gear.

Benji's gayness had lasted only as long as the fear. Once the storms cleared, he'd been adamant in his rejection. A friendship of years was smashed to pieces, as surely as if it had been dropped from the ledge to the park floor two thousand feet below.

Then he'd met Jake. Two years after Benji's hurtful words, Jake Landon had come into his life: handsome, intelligent, a little shy, and so damned sexy but not exactly aware of it, and a good thing too. He'd stolen Kurt's heart there in the little cabin without ever knowing, thinking instead that it was he who was being given the great gift. Kurt's heart beat a little faster at the thought of the moment by the lake when Jake had first kissed him and then shoved him into the water, just to get enough silence to say that he wanted Kurt as much as Kurt wanted him.

It wasn't just wanting, not now, not after five months that

they'd been together. Jake had followed him to Wapiti Creek, putting other life plans on hold to be where Kurt was. He hadn't said how long he could defer starting pharmacy school before they'd give his slot away, but he'd thrown himself into planning a resort winter, clearly not expecting to go this year, saying nothing about next year. There would be no avoiding a city life when he did go; Kurt would just have to cope with four years in Denver. He needed Jake to want him along.

Time to get off the lift. Kurt would find Rudi, tell him to shove his ski-pimping, and then call Jake. Maybe skiing with the little monsters wouldn't be so bad, and he'd get to be cooler than Jorey again. He scanned the short line for the second lift, not seeing the man, and not sure what colors he was looking for, anyway. Rudi would find him there at the entrance to the lift line.

Except here came Ulf, just exactly the man Kurt did not care to see. Smiling at him, for the first time ever. He didn't like Ulf, the pretentious ass, and he didn't trust Ulf, because he willingly participated in Rudi's little prostitution ring. The big skier in black swung down from Killy's Knees to halt by Kurt, followed by a gaggle of thirty-something women. They all gathered around the men, laughing and smirking at each other, as Ulf gave Kurt some bad news.

"Ah, Kurt, what you want is at top of mountain. I show you where."

At last. He'd get his hands on that miserable shit Rudi, and then he'd be done with Alpenschlössl. Kurt smiled widely, not caring that the future was becoming a bit uncertain financially.

The women all smiled back, like his grin was for them, and began to chatter. "Ulf! Introduce us!" demanded one of the well-groomed, expensively dressed flock.

"Kurt, this is Mandy, Leelee, Cassie, and Emily. My

students today." Ulf could be perfectly pleasant when he put his mind to it, Kurt thought as he shook hands with the ladies. Then he got mobbed.

Nearly knocked off his skis by women diving into his arms, he had to endure the exclamations. "Ooh, you're cute! Leelee, take a picture of us!" The woman in a metallic silver parka whipped out a fancy phone and aimed it at the little knot of people. "No, wait! I have to get one on each side!" Either Emily or Cassie—they were both in blue, and Kurt hadn't tried to keep them straight—inserted herself between Ulf and Kurt, grabbing their arms and grinning hugely, stepping on the tops of the men's skis to position herself.

"Have to do it again. Kurt, try not to grimace this time. Oh, fix Ulf's bandana, it's cockeyed." Everyone laughed, though the woman twitched the scarf around his neck into a better position. Leelee took another shot. "Dang it, Kurt! Look at the camera! You were looking down that time."

At the scratched tops of his skis, yeah. He tried to arrange his face pleasantly, but the nuisance grabbing his arm laid her head on his shoulder, smiling and posing for her friend to click again.

"Come on, Kurt! You can smile!" Leelee frowned over the top of the phone. "Or we're going to think you aren't glad to see us." She put the camera up again.

Ulf had his arm over EmilyorCassie's shoulder; he tapped Kurt's back hard. "*Ja*, smile."

Why would he be glad to see these women? He'd be more glad to see the backs of them, but they weren't going anywhere until this stupid photo session was done. Ulf was standing monolithically. He smiled, trying to get it all over with, but one of the other women squealed, "My turn! My turn!" and tried to push her friend out of the way.

The happier he looked, the sooner this would be over and they'd stop treating him like scenery. This time he put his arm over CassieorEmily's shoulder, since he'd gotten the other woman in blue, hoping to satisfy them before the storm blew completely in.

"Now me!" The third woman, Mandy, whose deep-rose jacket matched her sunburned nose, got her picture taken with the two men, and then Leelee handed her phone to one of the women in blue to step between them. Kurt smiled with gritted teeth through the various combinations of women in the pictures, letting them put their arms around his waist and snuggle up. Leelee even inveigled a passerby to take a picture of all four women with the men sandwiched between them. She slipped between Ulf and Cassie to smile into the lens as Emily and Cassie wiggled under Kurt's arms. He'd gotten light-blue jacket and dark-blue straightened out during the jostling in and out of the photographic field.

"Yuck, Emily, your lunch is going to show up in the pictures as a brown cloud!" Cassie shrank away from her friend, waving her hand in front of her face. "Lay off the Italian food, girl, it goes straight to your hips anyway."

"Sorry, Cass." Emily held her hand in front of her face, but Cassie pulled it down.

"Just smile, okay?" She turned a shining face to the photographer.

Kurt drew the line when she wanted kissing pictures.

"Cassie, the weather's going to turn before we get to the top of the mountain if we don't get moving," he suggested after she planted a juicy one on Ulf.

"Ooh! Anxious!" She giggled and winked at her friends. "Okay! Let's go!"

Yes, he was anxious. Rudi was up there somewhere, and he

needed to get this over with then get some lunch. Kurt led the way to the lift line, not noticing who was following.

"We talk together, ladies," Ulf told his class as he pushed up next to Kurt. "See you at the top," just wasn't enough to provoke the waves of giggles that followed the men up to the loading line to get to the top of the mountain. They were alone on the wide quad chair. Kurt suspected from the giggles that the four women on the chair behind them were going to have a dandy time.

Kurt sat down toward the middle of the seat, trying to take up the lion's share of the space, but Ulf had similar ideas. The big jerk sat nearer than Kurt would have liked, but he wasn't going to move over. He wouldn't acknowledge that Ulf could dominate him into moving. If Ulf didn't like the spacing, he could move his ass over.

Unfortunately, that was exactly what Ulf did. After they passed the second tower and had reached an elevation of perhaps forty feet, a drop that would injure, possibly kill, Ulf scooted over toward Kurt and put an arm over his shoulders, gripping him in place. Kurt whipped around to snarl but got kissed fiercely and passionlessly, and the left handed punch he aimed at Ulf's middle didn't carry enough momentum to end it.

"Fight for your virtue if you want," Ulf growled when he broke the kiss, "but your *Liebling* Jake will suffer for it."

"What the fuck?" Kurt gritted. "Let go of me!" The women in the chair behind were clearly entranced with what they were watching. He could see their mouths moving in "oohs" and "ahhs" even if he couldn't hear them.

"You listen." Ulf did not let go. At close range his breath was slightly sour, and his eyes were barely visible through his sunglasses. "You are Alpenschlössl teacher. You entertain the client."

"I quit. I've been telling Rudi that all day." Kurt punched at Ulf again, but the other instructor caught his arm in a grip that he couldn't break. He'd prefer the women thought he was cooperating rather than getting forced; he wouldn't struggle fruitlessly, but instead wait until he could make it count. The bar that came down over them, which should have kept them safe, was hindering his defenses.

"You sign contract, you do not quit. You went into this eyes open, knowing what is expected," Ulf said from closest range.

"I didn't know! That's why I want out." Kurt glared hard, but through the sunglasses, it had little effect on the big man who had him pinned. "I'm not a *huerä*."

"Such names you call. I explain again. If you do not cooperate here and now, for these ladies, your Jake will pay. *Tschäggsch es?*"

"I understand, all right," Kurt snarled. "You're a dead man if you touch him." He didn't care that the spittle flew as he promised retribution.

"Possibly I am and possibly I am not, but he will certainly have some interesting times first, *schafseckel.*" Ulf wiped his face with the hand that he incautiously took from Kurt's left wrist. Kurt slugged him again, harder, which doubled Ulf over enough to crack his forehead against his assailant's nose. Blood gushed all over Ulf, who stayed curled up against him in a parody of tenderness. The pain in Kurt's face froze him in place for a moment. Ulf grunted from the impact.

If the blood had been visible from behind, surely the women wouldn't have been saying, "Awww...." quite so loudly.

"Be a fool. The more you fight me, the worse it goes with

your lover. I would only help him to injury, but this has earned more." Ulf sat up straighter, pulling Kurt against him even harder. "I might give him this." He pulled Kurt's hand toward his crotch, placing it on something long, hard, but not flesh. Even through the gloves and other layers, the position, the angles, and the stiffness all told Kurt he had his hand on a gun. What sort, he didn't know, other than probably a nine millimeter semi-automatic, but even a twenty-two would be lethal at close range. His breath left him. "I don't have to kill, *schyssdrägg*."

Kurt froze, hearing the truth of that, his stomach churning as he thought of Jake broken and bleeding on his account. Ulf picked his head up and looked into Kurt's face.

"Or this." Ulf moved Kurt's hand farther up his leg, now, to his groin. "Disappoint this client in any way, and we learn if your happy man likes a *schoggi-schtooss* from me as much as he likes it from you." Ulf leaned forward to say this into Kurt's ear, both aping affection and hiding Kurt's suddenly pale face from the women. "Before or after I put bullet into him. You choose."

"Don't touch him!" Kurt wrenched himself out of Ulf's embrace, ready to vomit. "What do you want?" He ignored the cries of dismay behind them.

"We are a birthday gift to the pretty Cassie. She comes with us to the cabin, and her report to the other ladies decides if I have many clients or none. I want many. You understand?" Ulf drew him back in the seat and against his side, arm over his shoulder. Kurt allowed it, knowing only that he would have to protect Jake in any way he could. Even if it meant going along with what Ulf wanted him to do.

"You were a fool to come to Alpenschlössl," Ulf said, nuzzling Kurt's face to the cries of "Awww," from behind them.

He took his bandana off to wipe the blood that still trickled from Kurt's nose. "But you would be a bigger fool to leave just yet."

SIXTEEN

"Aw, you guys! What happened?" the women cried once they followed the men off the lift.

"Does the altitude give you nosebleeds?" Cassie grimaced as she looked at the blood. "Should we clean you up here?" She stole Ulf's bandana and scooped a handful out of the nearest snowbank. Fortunately, the blood in Ulf's pale blond hair attracted more of her attention than did Kurt's partially cleaned face—she began to scrub at his head. She was more than a head shorter than Ulf, so it was quite a reach.

"Thank you, dear, but we can clean up at our destination." Ulf cast glances at the other skiers going by, making the other women go into gales of "wink wink, nudge nudge" and giggles. Kurt thought he recognized people from the other night, but the big avalanche vests and the other equipment obscured them. If they were Mark and Marty, he wouldn't attract their attention.

"Ooh! Plumbing?" Emily giggled. "I didn't expect that!"

Into the babble of "have fun" and "see you later" Cassie said, "Wish me luck!" and turned to lead the group to the left of the lift. Only Killy's Knees and Cement Chute were marked on the map in that direction, with a "Closed" sticker over Cement Chute. Still, the entire group went that way, the three women stopping to watch Ulf take over the lead, breaking trail for Cassie and Kurt. Ulf glanced back—Kurt knew it was his warning to not cut and run down the other side. Grimly, he followed the two to a small A-frame cabin on the windward side of the mountain, over the rise from the slopes.

"Do not bring in the snow," Ulf warned as he unlocked the sliding glass door on the protected side of the A-frame. They left their skis on the porch, stuck in the snow that no one had cleared, though a set of tracks led both to and away from the porch. "Your key unlocks this, Kurt."

Great. Like he ever wanted to be here again. He didn't want to be here now, and only the total sincerity in Ulf's threats kept him from just bolting.

Cassie let Ulf help her off with her coat and then pulled off her ski boots in the little mudroom. She headed into the cabin as the men removed outerwear, exclaiming at the furnishings. "Oh, this is so cute!" She wandered through the one large room, around the fireplace, and returned smiling. "But cold! Yum! Lunch!" She peeked at a tray of finger foods and opened a container that steamed into the chill air. Kurt ducked to one side to avoid getting struck in the face with Ulf's parka. He got even by removing a ski boot that "accidentally" crashed into Ulf's shin.

"Yes," Ulf grunted, due to the timing of the ski boot, and then said sotto voce, "I bring Jake here sometime?"

Kurt pulled his other boot off without more contact. "Don't even think about it."

"Are you hungry?" Cassie popped a tiny quiche into her mouth and tried to feed Ulf a bite when he came into the tiny living room and kitchen area. He took the tidbit from her fingers with a smile. Kurt knew he would do the same, hungry or not. He had been thinking about lunch, but his appetite had fallen from the chairlift with Ulf's threats. "Here, sweetie." She stuck what might as well have been a rock into Kurt's mouth when he came into the living room. He chewed mechanically as he went to find the bathroom, which was in the one place it could reasonably be in this small cabin.

Ulf knelt to open a hidden door next to the central fireplace and twitched a valve open. "It will warm soon."

Not with that high A-frame roof, it wouldn't. Kurt glanced up to see a slightly vaulted, wooden eight-foot ceiling instead of a ceiling that matched the roofline— it probably would.

Flames began to dance on the gas log, making Cassie come to warm her hands by the wire mesh screen, sighing happily. "This is the only light, isn't it? It's so romantic!"

"Yes. No electricity here." Ulf shut the door to cover the barbecue-sized propane tank. "Though we do have water."

"Good. Go get the blood out of your hair, and do you guys have toothbrushes with you? I brought mine!" She whipped that article out of her pants pocket and brandished it.

There were new toothbrushes and some toothpaste laid out on the bathroom counter, Kurt had already discovered as he washed the blood from his face. Ulf had nailed him just right, creating a fountain, but breaking nothing. When he got the chance to return the favor, Kurt would make sure to break something for the fucker.

As he scrubbed his teeth, he looked around at the oddly appointed room. There was a sink, a commode, no shower or bath, but two things he hadn't seen in a bathroom outside of Europe. Ulf chased him out before he could turn the knobs, but his curiosity was his mind trying to defend him from the reality of his situation; he knew what a bidet was for, and the on-demand water heater would keep icicles from forming in anyone's crotch. The main room was getting warm now.

Ulf elbowed him out, and then Cassie slipped past, peeled down to just her long underwear, silky high tech, just not very sexy. Kurt took a deep breath, trying to prepare mentally for whatever came next. No matter what, he'd protect Jake.

"Fellas, don't we have way too many clothes on?" she asked brightly, after she'd brushed her teeth and combed out her hair, which fell in streaked "been braided a while" ripples to just below her shoulders. Cassie was standing near the king-sized bed with its brass bedstead, looking hopeful. She held out her arms to both men, and Ulf came to her with a smile.

Kurt came more slowly, trying to find a smile. While Ulf kissed her, Kurt worked to fix his face. The asshole had an arm around his shoulder as well as Cassie's, but Kurt could not force himself to put an arm around Ulf's waist. He needed the forti-tude for more difficult things.

Kissing Cassie could have been worse. She opened her mouth under Ulf's as Kurt nuzzled her neck and ear. Moaning and twisting as they mouthed her, finally she curled up against Ulf's chest, though she didn't let go of Kurt.

"I can't believe you guys are really here. I mean, wow, two hotties. I just keep thinking I'm dreaming, but...." She lifted hazel eyes to Kurt from the haven of Ulf's chest. "And I can hardly wait to see what you guys do together, I mean, it's like my big fantasy to see...."

If he had to play this game, he'd set some of the rules. "Then you'll love it when Ulf sucks my cock, Cassie, he's good, he's really into it, he wants it so bad, he's always on his knees." Kurt ignored Ulf's look of outrage aimed at him over Cassie's head, and spoke over her moaning. "And when I'm tired of him sucking, I'll turn him around so you can see how my cock goes in and out of his ass, he's so hot for that too—he screams for a *schoggi-schtooss*, he wants me to pound him until he can feel the head of my dick in his throat from behind, he's a maniac...."

Ulf tried to break in, but Kurt had tossed his chin at the moaning client who so clearly liked what she was hearing, and besides, Kurt could hope that the man's English was deserting him as he grew angrier. "I'll show you how much he likes it, our hot Swiss, he's such a slut, but he's fun. Oh, Cassie, you can't imagine, he's like the cheese, wants all his holes filled...."

Kurt kept talking in spite of the way Ulf was squeezing his shoulder. It hurt, but it wouldn't make him shut up: he'd keep Ulf from getting a word in edgewise. There'd be no contradicting Kurt without upsetting his client, the last thing Ulf wanted.

Kurt could play into her fantasies: "You want to see Ulf on his knees begging for it? Oh, Cassie, just tell him, he'll do it for you, he wants you to be so happy, just tell him what you want him to do, and he'll do it...." Kurt had started rubbing her back slowly, reaching down to grab her ass, kneading gently as he promised her all the delights of watching him ravage Ulf, because he was desperate not to be the one on his knees from either direction. If nothing else, he would salvage that much from this debacle.

"Oh, yeah, oh," she moaned, rubbing her face against Ulf's chest. Kurt somehow kept talking through the pain and brought his hand up to the side of Ulf's neck, where he hooked his fingers over the shoulder and dug them hard into the vulnerable area above the clavicle. The harder Ulf squeezed, the more Kurt talked and the harder he rammed his fingers into the painful spot. Jake had always told him he talked too much during intimate moments, but he sure wasn't shutting up now that he was gaining the upper hand. He filled Cassie's head with ideas.

"He's getting hard just thinking about what you and I are going to do to him, Cassie, just feel him." Kurt turned up the pressure from both hands and voice. Ulf let go of his shoulder, so Kurt stopped pushing on the pressure point. Ulf had to be able to fulfill the promises Kurt was making for him. There was another way to keep the big man silent. "Kiss him, Cassie, kiss him, he needs that, yeah, lots of tongue, kiss him…."

And on he talked. Cassie took her hand from Kurt's waist to touch Ulf's groin as she pulled him down to her mouth. Ulf glowered at Kurt as she groped him, but Kurt went on and on, practically forcing Ulf to will himself hard. Taking his arm away might help, though Kurt kept up his gentle caresses on her back as he murmured.

"I can't feel through the ski pants," Cassie grumbled after Kurt invented something else about Ulf's desires. "Need to get you undressed."

"Can't imagine why he isn't already naked with his ass up," Kurt agreed as Ulf shot daggers at him over Cassie's head. "Keep kissing him." He grinned evilly as she moaned; Ulf wanted him to make the client happy? Sure, but on his terms. Cassie bent her head down to look at the fasteners she struggled to undo at Ulf's waist, prompting Kurt to go on quickly with more details that Ulf could not contradict without annoying her.

Ulf mouthed, "I kill you," silently, but Kurt just went on, suggesting that Cassie should help prepare Ulf for what he would do. She gave up and pushed into Kurt's arms, back against him.

"Get naked, Ulf, come on, I want to see," she said, as she pulled Kurt's arms around her and held his hands, rubbing her ass against his groin. Roused from tormenting Ulf, Kurt's body responded to the pressure, making her moan a little more. "Oh, Kurt, you're already up. Who's bigger?"

"You'll have to check. Make Cassie happy, Ulf, do what she wants." Kurt leaned to nibble her ear as Ulf pulled clothing off, schooling his face into an approximation of horniness when Kurt was certain that the true mood was rage. If Ulf wasn't up, Kurt's house of cards might come tumbling down, with him underneath.

The tension made his diaphragm spasm, and the hiccup carried more than a hint of last night's feast.

"Ew, Kurt! I blamed the garlic on Emily, but it was you!" Cassie pulled away from him.

The cabin was at eleven thousand feet. Kurt's heart hit sea level. "Sorry."

"Me too. I can't deal with that, and we were going along so nicely." Cassie looked back and forth between the men.

Ulf emerged from his undershirt, aghast, as Kurt felt disaster for himself and his lover loom.

"You give such great voice, Kurt, you're just going to have to keep doing it, but from over here." She stepped over into Ulf's arms to press herself against the nearly naked man, whose bikini underwear covered a half-mast. He began to rub his hips against her, a furious attempt, Kurt guessed, to produce the promised erection. "You keep talking, get us back into the mood." She stopped and pursed her lips. "And then you need to go, because I don't want you to just watch us. We'll do it again tomorrow, all three of us, and Kurt—" She waggled her eyebrows menacingly. "You get oatmeal for dinner tonight, you got that? Nice, bland oatmeal."

"Can I put maple syrup on it?" Kurt humored her. She broke up in giggles.

There would be no tomorrow, if only that Rudi had booked the cabin and instructors elsewhere, though Kurt would be in Denver by then if he had to be. This wasn't like plumbers returning a second day to finish a project.

Her instructions were the first he'd gotten that pleased him: he wanted nothing so much as to leave. If it didn't occur to her that he and Ulf could screw with her out of garlic range, or if that just wasn't her fantasy, he wasn't about to bring it up. He'd provide stage directions for the other two actors before exiting stage left and putting a couple of miles of snow between them. He pitched his voice again to sensuality.

"Then kiss him, Cassie, he needs to feel your mouth on him, run your hands over his skin, doesn't he feel good, strong and hard? Yeah, keep touching him, grab his ass, yeah, both hands, he likes his ass played with, feel the muscles in there flexing, Ulf's got nice hard buns, keep grabbing him...."

Kurt could keep this up all day if it kept him out of reach and still satisfied Ulf. The man was bent over enough to kiss her, though he could flick his glance up at his adversary, and his eyes were full of hate. "Skier's thighs, Cassie, can you grab them? They're like tree trunks. How's his dick, Cassie? Getting hard for you?"

It should be if Ulf was responding to his client at all, because she was one horny, happy woman, worming into his arms. She still had her long jills on, but Kurt would direct them to strip in a moment, get them under the covers so that he could make his escape without further annoying Cassie with the blast of cold air from the door. The cabin was warm enough for nudity, he thought, sweating inside his clothing. He'd removed nothing except the ski boots and his outerwear, so he could jump into the boots and fasten everything once he was outside. He kept talking as he edged toward the door.

"Mmmm, Ulf, isn't our Cassie so warm and cuddly? Don't you just have to take every stitch of clothes off her to see? Her skin's so soft, I wish I could touch her, you touch her, you tell me how she feels, wow, you can almost span her waist with your hands, she's yummy...." With smiling approval, Kurt watched Ulf follow his instructions. "Get under the goose down, keep her warm. Oh yeah, you two are gorgeous...." He stuffed his feet into his boots. "Shame to cover up all that lusciousness, but it's going to get cold here in a second." He shrugged into the coat, spinning more lies. "You guys have a great time, I'd love to be in that bed with you, gonna eat nothing but oatmeal until I see you again."

He was out the sliding door in a flash, dropping a glove in his haste. Bent to grab it, he saw the pair in the bed on the far side of the room, Cassie apparently on top of Ulf. They were visible only as a moving lump under the goose down, aside from the large, masculine hand aiming an upthrust middle finger his way.

Can't say he didn't leave the client happy, he thought, clipping into his bindings. It would be a slight uphill trudge back on piste, then he'd blow down Killy's Knees and find Jake. And Rudi. There would be no repeats of this shit.

SEVENTEEN

I groped for my phone, patting every one of the way too many pockets this parka and pants had. No phone. Damn. Mr. Underwood should have asked for a number for emergencies, then I would have known way earlier that I'd left the damned thing on the charger again. I hoped Kurt would think to find me at the bunny lift. I ignored Egon studiously as he warned the loading skiers that this would be their last trip up the hill today.

"We had such fun, Daddy!" Gracie prattled to her father, who was sailing in from Galloping Goose.

Todd chimed in. "Jake is really good! He wants to go on the black diamonds tomorrow!"

"Then he'll go without you, kids. Nice try." Mr. Underwood looked at me. "Good time had by all?" Melanie arrived about then, looking exhausted in the fading light. Dark comes early and fast in the mountains in November.

"Yes, sir. On blues and greens." I shot a quelling look at Todd before he tried to throw me under the bus again. Self-centered kid. Not to mention I didn't belong on the black diamonds.

"Good. Let's head home, kids, we have guests tonight." Mr. Underwood turned to his wife. "Ready, honey?"

They left me standing by the lift, hoping that Kurt would come along. If he didn't show soon, I was going to freeze in place, so I'd go home and wait for him there while I got dinner ready. Flakes were already starting to come down. I'd heard forecasts of twelve to fifteen inches. It made me glad to not be a snowcat driver after all: they'd be at work by 3 a.m. to make the snow all perfect for the skiers. I intended to be curled next to Kurt in a warm bed at that ungodly hour.

"Hey, Jake!" A voice behind me made me turn around.

"Hey, Mark. What's with all the gear?" He looked like an alien with a pack bulking up his shoulders and running behind his head and things attached to tool belts.

"Marty and I were in the back country, doing snow tests. This is an inflatable vest, in case we get caught in an avalanche. It should keep us at the surface of the snow. Lot of whumpfing today." He patted the vest. "Thought I might need it for real."

"Whumpfing?" I laughed.

"The sound of nature screaming that the snowpack is unstable. The storm tonight will probably open the back bowls on the east side, and Cement Chute might slide without our help." He loosened the straps. "What are you doing tonight?"

I thought we'd had this part clear before. "Waiting for Kurt."

Mark looked troubled. "Doesn't his job bother you?"

"He doesn't have that job any more. He quit." Hell, yes, it bothered me, but I was going to spread the word that he and Alpenschlössl parted ways instead of discussing it.

"About that...." Mark cleared his throat. "Do you know where he was today?"

"He taught a lesson on an intermediate slope, and then he planned to spend the rest of the day having a good time skiing." Maybe he'd met up with someone who could keep up with him. I didn't see the problem.

"Well, if that's what he told you...." He turned to go.

I grabbed his arm. "Spill it, Mark." I did not like the implication that my open, honest Kurt had done something sneaky.

"I don't want to be the one to tell you, Jake." He tried to yank his arm back. "You'll just think I'm making it up."

"Tough. Just say." My gut churned. I'd had enough of everybody knowing but us. Or me.

He broke free from my gloved hand. "Okay. Marty and I rode up the lift behind him. He was acting really friendly with Ulf. The other Alpen—"

"I know who Ulf is!" I broke in.

"And at the top, there were a bunch of women with them. One went with them to that cabin. We saw them go in, and then we went back of the cornice, and I don't know what happened after that." He looked off to one side. "I'm sorry. But you asked."

I had. I was sorry I had. I trusted Kurt. I knew what he'd told me. I'd heard him on the phone, yelling at Rudi's voice mail. But Mark sounded so sincere. I was ready to tell him he was right, that he had to be making it up just to have a chance with me, when someone pulled up.

"Shit, Mark." It was Marty, whom I could barely identify in my turmoil. "You told him, didn't you? Jerk."

I looked blankly at him, noticing only that he was as decked with equipment as his partner.

"I'm sorry, Jake." Marty put his hand on my shoulder.

"Maybe there was a good explanation for them going to the cabin."

I just couldn't imagine what it would be. I threw up one hand aimlessly; words weren't coming. Mark had said it. Marty had confirmed it. Marty, who had no interest in me, no ulterior motive.

"Maybe." I got that much out.

"Come on, let's get you inside," Marty said. "You're probably tired, cold, and hungry and all of this sounds worse than it is. There's hot chocolate inside." They guided me to the staff hut, and we left our skis in the lockers outside.

"I'll take your stuff to the office." Mark took Marty's gear and left me alone with him. Other skiers came to drop things off.

"Sit down." Marty guided me to a table in the dining room. "I'll be right back." He returned with steaming cups, which he set down in front of us. "This will help." The slugs of liquid he poured from the flask into each cup smelled like peppermint. "It's okay, drink." Marty just sat quietly, watching me.

I did drink it, but more because I'd been told to than from wanting it. I didn't want anything except for things to roll back to what they'd been this morning, when the world was bright and Kurt was the sun. The dark looked in the windows to the room, bright with electricity. Was Kurt's brightness equally false?

"I'll stay with him, Marty. Chelsea's waiting for you." Mark had found us.

"Jake, don't make any decisions until you talk to him. There's probably more to this than you know yet." I hated Marty for reading my mind. I didn't look up as he left, just poked the handle of the cup to make it lurch around in a slow circle on the table. Something passed from one to the other. I didn't look up to see what it was. "Get some more cocoa into him; he looks shocky." There was a pressure on my shoulder and silence.

Mark stole my cup, leaving me nothing to poke except for my sad thoughts. Everything I thought was certain in the world about me and Kurt was now in doubt. I didn't know what I'd do. I couldn't imagine what he could tell me about what had surely happened that would make it all okay. Last night he'd been mine, and today he was... what? I couldn't breathe from the constriction in my chest, and I wasn't sure I wanted to.

"Don't play with it, just drink." Mark's hand was probably supposed to be comforting against my back, but it was one more thing I couldn't cope with, even to shrug it away.

I reached a forefinger to the cup handle again when it reappeared in my field of vision. More peppermint trickled into it, stinging my nose and then burning my throat when I drank it to the dregs, just to make Mark be quiet. I'd made Kurt be quiet now and then. How many times had I told him to shut up when he needed to say something important? I set the cup down and didn't even try to focus when it went a bit fuzzy. It wasn't worth the effort.

Damn it! Jake was just as hard to get a hold of as Rudi. He'd left the phone on the charger again, no doubt. A week of carrying it wasn't enough to break the habit of not needing it. Kurt stuffed the phone back into his own pocket, trying to match Jake's thought process. They'd parted ways at the bunny lift, where he'd collected the Walkers and Jake could have reasonably collected the kids. It was about four thirty; he might as well try there, and just head home if he couldn't find his lover.

The base of the bunny lift was also where Egon lurked. The bastard was there now.

"You look for Jake?" Something was tickling Egon—Kurt could see the grin even from this distance. This just had to be his day for assholes.

"Yeah," he called back, wondering why Egon would be so helpful.

"Try staff hut," he yelled back, and went back to loading the last few skiers.

Sounded reasonable. Kurt kicked off in that direction, drawn by the brightly lit windows. Jake kept his skis there in the lockers overnight, and it would be warmer than standing in the falling snow.

Kurt went cold, though, from what he saw through the window in the dining room. Jake sat over a cup of something with Mark, who looked earnestly into his face, touching his arm, and Jake let him do it. Had today been all for nothing?

EIGHTEEN

"You are a cheap date." Mark had my arm over his shoulder to steer me through the door and up the stairs. "You didn't have that much."

Two? Three? Hot chocolate and peppermint sat on my tongue. It was schn—, shn—whatever, mint. They'd thrown us out of the staff hut after about an hour. "Said I wasn't mush of a drinker." I stumbled on the step.

"No kidding." Mark paused at the top of the stairs. "Jake, do you want to see him like this?" He had both hands on my shoulders. I wobbled anyway. "You might say something you'll regret."

I thought about that. "S'all regrets." Had to grab onto him to stay upright.

"Can't be. But you could stay with me until you sober up."

He looked pretty good, never told me lies. Maybe get only truth out of that wide mouth. Maybe get kisses. Maybe get something... into that wide mouth. I toppled into his arms.

"Nope, there is no way I can get you up another flight of stairs. Come on, stand."

Okay, wasn't *that* sloshed. I let him balance me and aim me down the hall. He pulled up at the door and knocked. Kurt opened after a moment. Wasn't glad to see me. Was mutual. I waved at Mark with the arm that wasn't around his neck. "You 'member Mark?"

"I assume there is a good explanation for this?" Kurt caught me as I stumbled through the door toward the couch. He tipped me toward the furniture. I poured onto the cushions. World was a little whirly.

"I think that was what he planned to say to you, before he got into the peppermint schnapps. It hit him hard." Mark sounded like he didn't like Kurt. I didn't like Kurt right now. Liar.

"He never drinks." Kurt shoved me over so both butt cheeks were on the couch and started pulling my coat off. "Were you feeding it to him?"

"Only because he was shocky."

Kurt turned hard eyes on my new buddy. Wanted to tell him to stop.

"He found out where you'd spent your afternoon."

"Courtesy of you?"

Mark nodded. I nodded too, made my head swim.

Kurt growled at him. "I thought that was you at the top of the lift. Let me tell you something, *pal,* he doesn't know the whole story and neither do you. So don't tell him things you don't know shit about."

"I know he deserves better than an Alpenschlössl whore."

Was magic—Kurt moved his arm, Mark folded over like our dining room table.

"If I *was* an Alpenschlössl whore, he'd deserve better than me!" Kurt pulled Mark upright.

Mark popped Kurt under the chin. Was hard to see his hand going that fast. "You went to the cabin with them."

Kurt's head wasn't s'posed to go back like that. "I quit! But Ulf made me—" He made Mark double again. Watching made me queasy. Should tell them to stop. "He threatened—" Mark's fist pushed the words back into Kurt's mouth. Hey, I was only one who could tell Kurt to shut up.

"Right, it wasn't your fault. It's never anybody's fa—" Mark hit the floor. Kurt jumped on him. Wai' minute, Kurt's s'posed to pounce on me.

"Damn you! Listen!" Thud, Mark's head bouncing on floor. "That sick fuck Ulf said he'd hurt Jake bad if I didn't go!" Kurt rolled away. Leaned on couch. Close enough to touch. Didn't. "I don't know why I'm explaining to you."

Mark sat up. "You want me to believe you were protecting him, not stepping out on him." Touched the back of head. "Because I'm the guy who wants a chance with him."

Kurt jerked up. Looked mean. "Don't even think about it."

"I think about it a lot. Although he doesn't look like much of a prize at the moment." I bleared at him. Tha' wasn't nice. "Back to Ulf…."

"That dude is fucking insane. The things he said he'd do to Jake…." Kurt slumped over. Wished I could move enough to pet him. World kind of fuzzed in and out.

"… bad. I can see it." Why was Mark sitting next to Kurt? Why's his arm over Kurt's shoulders? Wanted to kick him. Couldn't. Couldn't keep eyes open.

NINETEEN

I woke up in the morning, head aching. The night had been horrible. The evening had been worse, and what was more, there seemed to be chunks missing.

Kurt was missing too. I got up off the couch where I'd landed the night before, pushing the blanket away. He must have covered me, but that was a missing chunk. This was the first night I hadn't spent touching him in some way since he'd come home after the fire. Bad things danced at the edges of my memory: things with Kurt, things with Mark. Things with Mark and Kurt. A shower would clear my head.

Where was I supposed to be today? The spray washed enough clarity into me that I remembered being off, comp time for taking the boss's kids skiing. Okay, time enough to figure out what was going on. I rubbed the towel over my hair, wondering where Kurt was and if he could fill in some of my blanks. Or if he would. Not trusting Kurt was one of the things I did remember.

That hurt. That really hurt, because I had let my guard down for him, letting him into my heart like no one else, ever.

"There's more to this than you know" echoed in my head. Someone had said that, but the words bounced hollowly off the knowledge that he'd told me one thing and done another. Gone to the cabin with Ulf and a girl, that part stuck only too well with me.

Threatened, someone had been threatened, but was that Mark? Kurt had punched him, but he'd punched back. Couldn't remember. Did remember some unauthorized hugging on Kurt. Was Mark moving in on him? No, he was moving in on me. I thought. Did remember hanging around his neck on the way home.

I was never going to get drunk again. I really was a cheap date.

My head had hurt with the tapping of keys in the night. I'd hidden from the light and the sound under a pillow, which Kurt must have provided as well; it usually lived on the bed. I carried it back into the bedroom to replace it on the bed, neatly made as per Kurt's usual, showing no signs that I'd ever slept in it. Showing no sign that I hadn't slept in it last night. The only sign that Kurt might have slept in it was the gray wool sock that stuck out from under the bed. I picked it up, intending to throw it in the basket the way I'd thrown so many of his wandering socks, but I couldn't let it go.

I couldn't let Kurt go. Sitting on the edge of the bed with his sock in one hand, I told myself that Kurt always, always, had good reasons for what he did, and I hadn't heard him out. There were things he'd said last night while he and Mark pounded each other that I couldn't remember. I'd told him to shut up more times than I could recall, but now I'd have to find him and ask him to tell me. Sometimes I'd stopped his words with kisses, but I'd have to hope that there would still be kisses after I heard his words this time.

Carrying the sock, I wandered into the kitchen, where the coffee was still warm and a piece of paper stuck out from under the bottle of aspirin.

Gone to the mountain
K

There were a lot of reasons why he might have gone to the mountain, I thought as I swallowed some of both. I just hoped he didn't break his neck pounding down a hill looking for the comfort that he might have expected to get from me.

I dressed for the slopes, Kurt's stray sock paired with one of mine. It was only at the staff hut, stepping into my bindings, that I realized my phone was still on the charger.

The trouble with Wapiti Creek was that it was a damned big ski area. Two peaks, eight lifts, plenty of terrain for the relative handful of skiers who could afford to come here. It all made for a wonderful vacation experience but ultimate frustration for someone who needed to find one skier on the slopes. I thought back to where Kurt and I had spent the most time and concluded that the Scott lifts were my best bet.

I wanted a warm-up and some information, so I started at the bunny hill, thinking I'd get a running start at the Lower Scott lift and maybe some information.

"Seen Kurt or Mark this morning?" I asked Egon, who shook his head. The chair swooped under me before I could ask anything else. He wasn't exactly reliable, though Tom and Cynthia at the top of the hill gave the same negative answer.

I didn't know the operators at the Lower Scott and didn't have time to educate them on who I was looking for—they motioned me to get moving or get out of line. I would have to fix this social isolation, though the wonderful results so far didn't inspire me. Kurt wasn't there, and waiting a while didn't produce him. I went up the hill and came down Sugar Gulch, thinking that loitering a while at the junction with Dynamite Alley might be useful.

I blew down Sugar Gulch, reveling in the fresh powder that had fallen overnight, looking for untracked places where I would be the first to mark the snow. The powder hushed the mountain. My skis only swished on the snow, and the light breeze in the trees rubbed the pine needles together and made the frozen branches creak. When I stopped at the junction, my skis threw up the powder, making a little storm just for me with the crystals that fell back away from the impossibly blue Colorado sky.

I peered to the top of Dynamite Alley, wishing for every red and black speck I saw to grow into the form of my beloved, but three went by and not one was Kurt. I was getting cold, so I left my watching station, thinking that enough runs emptied at the Lower Scott that he might well come through there.

If he'd wanted to talk to me, he could have wakened me this morning. But he'd left me on the couch, asleep and ignorant. My thoughts grew bleaker with the wait.

"Jake!" I was jolted out of staring at the nearly hypnotic stream of skiers that were not Kurt going by. The voice was young, piping, and happy, and belonged to my little friend Gracie. "Come ski with us!" Her family trailed in her wake.

"Gracie, not just now." I did not want to be distracted from my search. Todd grabbed my hand and pulled on it, adding to his sister's plea.

"You really are her favorite," Melanie said. "I don't know why she likes you so much." She pulled her long brunette hair out of her jacket, twisted it around a few times and tucked it back in.

Because I pay attention to her. "I'm waiting for Kurt."

"Oh." Gracie's face fell.

"Glad to see you, Jake. It would be nice if you could do a run or two with the kids." Great, my über-boss wanted another chunk of my time off. Saying no didn't seem to be an option when the request came from him. Mr. Underwood lifted his eyebrow, waiting for the automatic agreement.

"You and Mrs. Underwood want to hit the black diamonds then?" I figured that would bring howls from the kids and might get me out of it.

"We're still trying to master one of the intermediates. I'm beginning to wonder about that instructor my wife hired." Melanie blanched behind him. The twins had started to bounce at the mention of black diamonds, but settled.

"We go faster than Mama does. Come with us, Jake. Please?" That little girl had big brown eyes and long lashes; it wasn't fair to take off her goggles and bat them at me. I might be impervious to her charms, but Daddy responded, right on cue.

"We'll collect them at eleven here, Jake." Mr. Underwood clapped me on the shoulder. "Good man. Let's go." He and his wife led the way into the lift line.

I recognized a situation I could neither influence nor change. With one five-year-old on each hand, I followed, wondering again at being drafted as babysitter.

"How was dinner with the team last night?" I asked, and the kids were off and running. I heard all about playing soccer with a foam ball in the living room with Jorey and playing checkers with Ted, and the kids took care of all the conversational needs of an entire chairlift ride while I said, "yeah, uh huh," in the right places, and they were happy.

Once at the top of the lift, I seized control of the skiing, something that I'd had trouble with before. "Let's do *S* today! Sugar Gulch or Sundance first?"

"Which one's steeper?" Todd asked with a gleam in his eye, but we chose Sundance because Gracie liked the name.

Untracked snow was getting harder to come by, but the kids carved their way through the little we found, and the silence that marked my earlier runs was broken now by laughter. Once the little brats went around a curve far ahead of me, having dared me to a version of hide and seek that was more like catch-up, and pelted me with snowballs when I came around the bend. I got them back as they came downhill toward me—they had to watch me make my ammunition. Yipping and evading the missiles, they raced back to the lift line, eager to try it all over again.

I looked around for Kurt, but he wasn't ahead of us. The red and black figure coming downhill might be him, but there were at least three others on this part of the mountain, and I didn't want to get my hopes up too far. I tried not to look as the kids and I planned our next run, debating Sugar Gulch or Prospector.

The word was usually a request to join strangers on a ski lift. My heart twisted as a familiar voice behind me said, "Single?"

I turned to look into blue eyes. "I hadn't planned to be."

TWENTY

Kurt put his sunglasses back on before he responded, and there was a catch in his voice. "Do you think we could discuss it first?"

My little chaperones hovered protectively around me, realizing that the laughter had fled. They stared solemnly at Kurt. Todd grabbed the shaft of my ski pole, and Gracie leaned against my leg.

"Yeah, except I've got—" I grabbed her before she fell all the way, her skis going out from under her as she pressed against me. I managed to get her upright, though nearly pulling her pink parka over her head. "—the kids."

"Don't lean back over the tails of the skis like that," Kurt advised her. I pulled the jacket down, and her face peeked out of the hood again. "You want to keep your feet a little farther apart and your weight a little forward. It will make you go faster too." He tipped her to the improved position.

"Faster than Todd?" she wanted to know.

"You have to show me too!" demanded the little competitor, and just like that, it was certain that Kurt would join us.

"So, how did you get to ski with the junior racers?" Kurt asked over Gracie's head, once we settled in the quad chair for a ride halfway up the mountain.

"Mr. Underwood elected me." My voice was wry, and the kids picked up on my reluctance.

"You said you wanted to find Kurt and here he is. Aren't you happy to ski with all of us?" Gracie's lower lip quivered.

Damn it, I was not going to make a kid cry. "It's my best and only choice, Gracie." She only looked partly comforted, and I wasn't comforted at all, because there wasn't much Kurt and I could talk about with the kids along.

"Sometimes there is only one choice." Kurt faced straight ahead, his eyes hidden by the curve of his sunglasses. "Because the alternative doesn't bear thinking about." He had his poles in one hand and the other gripped the safety bar until I could nearly hear the tendons twanging through his gloves.

A misty recollection from last night of "that sick fuck Ulf" floated through my brain. I couldn't remember what Kurt had said, though. His mouth was swollen and lopsided—had Ulf hit him?

"What's 'alternative'?" Todd piped up. He had been paying entirely too much attention, though I'd thought he was busy ogling all the Mardi Gras beads hanging in the trees along the lift.

"It's the other when you have a choice of one or the other," Kurt said.

"Well, what's the alternative now?" Todd went on. "Ski with us or not ski with us?"

"There is no alternative now. I'm skiing with you." I shuddered to think where the kids could end up. Would the lift operators at the Upper Scott keep them off if they showed up alone in line?

"Why? You don't really want to." Dratted kid was too perceptive.

"That doesn't matter. It wouldn't be safe otherwise." How do parents ever win an argument? At least I could eventually hand this crew back to their proper keepers.

Kurt took off his glasses and looked over at me again. "Sometimes," he said, and there was pain in his voice, "there is nothing more important than keeping someone else safe." He paused. "*Nothing.*" I'd never seen pleading in his eyes before, but he pleaded with me now, to understand, maybe to forgive.

Any details that might go with "sick fuck" were not details I could ask for now. Kurt did everything for a reason, I reminded myself. I briefly considered shoving the kids off the chairlift so I could find out.

"Right," I agreed with him, and some of the tension ran out of his shoulders. "So we ski together."

Our run down Sugar Gulch was punctuated by lots of stops and gentle instruction. "Okay, Todd, shift a little more forward and move your shoulders this way—" Kurt paused to move the little boy's body. "—when you turn. Like this, when you turn the other way." It was a more innocent version of my last ski lesson. I had to look away from the group as I remembered.

"Pay attention, Jake!" Gracie was a bossy little thing! "Or we'll beat you 'cause you won't know how to do it!" I snapped back to watch, wondering how long until eleven. Todd launched downhill and stopped after three turns. Gracie followed, waiting with her brother as Kurt showed me what he meant.

"Whatever you're imagining about yesterday, it wasn't like that," he murmured as he moved my shoulders. I couldn't bear to think again about my imaginings—I poled off and got two turns in before stopping just downhill of the kids.

"Pretend you've got poles and they mustn't drag," Kurt suggested, all business again, demonstrating the technique. "You've gotten used to letting your arms dangle, and you need them for balance and turns." Down the slope we went, Kurt trailing and watching.

The last half of the run was just pleasure. Kurt offered encouragement from behind us, and the mountain was mine to carve as I found what had been missing in my balance. The junction with Dynamite Alley came up, so we stopped and looked uphill to see what might be running us down.

Skiers in blue and white parkas were coming down that hill in pairs spaced at wide intervals. The kids waved madly, shrieking, "Tom! Jorey! Nick!"

Some went by with smiles, others with waves, and one pulled out of the speeding lineup just below us. "Hey, guys!" We stayed to the side as we joined Jorey. "Are you having a good time?"

"Kurt's teaching us to ski like you!"

"Kurt better not be teaching you to ski like me! If you do that, people will say things about cats on ice." Jorey laughed, rubbing the top of Todd's head.

Gracie tried that out, "paws" scrabbling wildly. "Raaaaawwwr!" She fell in a heap of giggles.

"Like that." He picked her up and pointed uphill. "Watch Ted. Kurt will teach you how to do it like Ted." There was a noticeable difference in style; Jorey had stuck out as the wild man in this swift, graceful crowd.

"But you're going to beat Ted at Kvitfjell, you said so. So we should ski like you." Todd stuck his lip out. Another adult bested by kid logic. I felt better, watching Jorey try to puzzle this one out.

"Tell you what, you ski fast like me, with technique like

Ted. And Ted is going to try to beat me, you know." Jorey looked satisfied with his answer and confident that Ted wasn't going to succeed. "'The best and fastest way to learn a sport is to watch and imitate a champion.' Jean-Claude Killy said that, and he knew—he was a champion when your dad was a kid."

"But wouldn't Ted beat you if he skied more like you?" Todd suggested. Another graceful racer whipped by.

"Ted's a champion too. He won gold gold medals. You ask hard questions, mister." Jorey ended the discussion by picking Todd up and swinging him upside down, skis waving. "I'm going to drop you in a snow bank!"

He damned near dropped the kid out of sheer surprise at the screams. Kurt was there before I was, grabbing Todd's hands and pulling him upright, setting him on his feet as Jorey let go, white-faced.

"Hey, buddy, you used to like that. What happened?"

Todd clutched Kurt's waist, shaking, but no longer sounding like a siren.

"That was before he nearly took a header off a chairlift," Kurt told him. I had hold of Gracie, who had also screamed a bit, probably just to keep Todd company in the noise department.

"That was you? Todd, buddy, I'm sorry. I didn't mean to scare you." Todd glared at Jorey with deep suspicion. The last of the racers sailed by, yelling at Jorey. "I gotta go. You have fun." He picked up momentum, but the others still had the speed from the hill, and Jorey trailed them. He kept looking over his shoulder at us, which couldn't have helped him catch up.

Kurt patted Todd's shoulder and then gently rubbed his back. "You okay there?"

"Yeah." Todd didn't let go of Kurt until Jorey was a speck at the lift line.

"We'll go when you're ready," Kurt told him, and I nodded when Todd looked to me.

"I don't want to ski like Jorey anymore. I want to ski like Ted." Todd stuck his chin out and then grinned at Kurt. "And you." Kurt grinned back.

I tried to disentangle myself from Gracie and get turned around. She slithered by me, and I slipped backward, center of gravity going somewhere it shouldn't have gone. I ended spread eagled in the snow. Wiping the powder off my face, I looked up to see the kids pointing and howling, and Kurt trying hard not to laugh.

The brat added, "But not like Jake!" and took off for the lift line pell-mell, followed by a pink blur.

"He has a point there, Jake." Kurt lost the battle with the belly laugh as he helped me up off the snow. I grimaced at him and started after my charges, hoping they didn't get halfway up the mountain without me. They stayed entertained in the lift line by having a miniature snowball fight with the snow we pulled out of my clothing, and we were about a third of the way up the hill when we all went silent.

I looked at Kurt and Kurt looked at me; we weren't much closer to getting things worked out than we had been before. The kids had insinuated themselves between us so we couldn't talk, except in a roundabout manner, and I didn't even know how to start that, so the ride was pretty quiet. Kurt broke the silence once. "I told Rudi I was going to go public if he didn't meet me."

There was nothing I could say to that in front of the kids, though I had a thousand questions still. So all I said was, "Good."

"Prospector this time?" I asked once we'd offloaded. We had time for another couple of runs.

"Prospector is narrow, so we'd have to go one at a time, and it will be hard to show you guys stuff on that one," Kurt pointed out. "It's probably not the best run for us."

"Let's do Prospector." Gracie trembled under my hand. "Kurt, please don't ski with us this time."

"Why?" Kurt looked stunned.

"You say something and Jake stops laughing." She wrapped her hands around my forearm. "You make Jake sad, and I don't like that."

I was trying to not make people shut up so much, but I'd really started with the wrong example because I couldn't argue with her reasoning.

"Me, either." Todd had switched loyalties again.

"I don't like it, either," Kurt said. "We have to fix that."

I was all for rolling the kids downhill in a barrel, just so we could be alone to do that, but Gracie went on. "You should do that when he isn't skiing with us."

"Yeah, you're right." Kurt quirked one side of his mouth, reminding me how long it had been since I'd seen his dimple. About twenty-four hours, but it seemed like years. "Catch you later, Jake." He swung away and was gone, even though I called his name.

"Stick around the Scott lifts!" I bellowed down the mountain, though I couldn't be sure he'd heard. The kids hunched up small as I turned around again, but I got a grip on my wrath.

"Chasing my friend away isn't how to get me to laugh again," I told them, as gently as I could. Inside, I ached; Kurt and I needed to talk, make things all right, make me understand completely what I only understood dimly now.

"You weren't laughing before, you aren't laughing now. What's the difference?" Todd grumbled, and took off without really watching where he was going, because he headed down a green slope that none of us enjoyed.

I thought we would have to wait a while for the Underwoods, because we got to the base of the lift a little early. Once again I would be reduced to hunting for Kurt needle-in-a-haystack style, because I couldn't remember his phone number. Once I'd programmed it into my autodial, it was out of my memory. Nine seven zero, followed by seven missing digits. I was debating going back home for my phone when the Underwoods showed up.

"Thanks, Jake. Good time had by all?" Mr. Underwood looked dubiously at our three long faces. "By anyone?"

"Intermittently. We had a pretty good snowball fight," I prompted them, and the kids didn't disappoint.

"Yeah, we did, and we got a ski lesson from Kurt—"

"That's Jake's friend, and—"

"We saw Ted and Jorey with the team—"

"Jorey says Kurt was teaching us to ski like Ted—"

The kids interrupted each other wildly as the stories tumbled out, making Mr. Underwood look approvingly upon me once again. "I heard there was a former US Ski Team member teaching on the mountain. Would that be Kurt?"

"Yes, it would." I began to wonder if there wasn't something useful to Kurt's future lurking in this conversation.

"If you see him, tell him I'd like to talk to him." He collected his family, and before he headed off, he added darkly, "That clown who's been teaching Melanie isn't worth a damn."

That sounded like either a plum job in the making or another disaster. Either way, it wasn't "if" I saw Kurt, it would be "when." I just had to go find him again.

TWENTY-ONE

If Kurt didn't turn up in a fairly short time, I'd go back to the apartment and fetch my phone. Heaven help the fool who got in my way now. Mr. Underwood had the clout to distract me, possibly my boss Roy did, and anyone else was going to get chewed up and spit out.

The run down Sundance was to get me to the bottom of the Lower Scott lift, not to enjoy, and I did it fast. A couple of the runs leading off the Upper Scott fed to the lower lift, a few to the upper lift, so I had to check both. I was getting frustrated and ready to fetch the phone when I ran across Gabe, swinging past the bottom of the high mountain lift. I hailed him, wondering if he knew anything helpful.

"How'd you get here so fast?" he asked.

"I'm picking up speed," I told him, with just a touch of pride. "I think I've cut about ten minutes off Sundance."

"No, weren't you up at the top of the higher lift? I thought that was you." He looked at me oddly. "Heading off with that Alpenschlössl guy."

"I'm trying to find him, actually." I was too frustrated and anxious to learn more to argue with him about calling Kurt "that Alpenschlössl guy."

"What would you want with Ulf?" Gabe looked ready to spit. "He's an asshole."

"I don't want Ulf. I want Kurt!" Damn it, one more dead end!

"You find Ulf, you'll find Kurt. He came along a little after you—or whoever—and Ulf did, and Ulf asked me to tell him that you were with him. So I did." Gabe looked at me sideways. "Mark asked about you too, when he and Marty went by. I don't get it."

"I do. Thanks, Gabe." I whacked his arm lightly and hauled off to the lift line. There was a large yellow sign with black lettering to warn me that I was heading into expert terrain, but I'd head into the jaws of hell if I had to. As Kurt said, sometimes nothing was more important than keeping someone safe.

Ulf was luring Kurt into a trap, and I was the bait.

On the way up, I wondered what I could do to get Kurt out of whatever Ulf had planned. Physically I might be a match for Ulf, athletically I wasn't, but I'd settle for driving him off and resolving matters later on level ground. If sheer fury could melt the snow around him, I'd leave him to drown in the flood it would cause, but I needed a better plan. Unfortunately, I had no way to plan, no weapons, no knowledge of the terrain above me, nothing but desperation and ski gear. It would have to be enough.

Find them first. The map at the top of the lift had a "Closed" sticker covering up most of Cement Chute, and Killy's Knees and off-piste territory were the only other things marked to the west. The cabin Mark had mentioned had to be over here, because that ridge had what looked like a cornice, if I understood right, and I'd just have to see what I could see when I got there.

"Killy's Knees only down that way!" yelled the lift attendant. I waved without looking, yeah, sure, and kept going anyway. Tracks diverged: the beaten path went one way and a barely broken track made by only one or two skiers went the other.

The snow was pristine in this treeless area, other than the narrow path that didn't look like many people had passed that way. Tracks of skis went down a bit and then up into a small climb, where the wind was starting to sift the snow into the herringbone path that led up the rise. People on alpine skis had gone up that hill.

I was betting there was a love-nest cabin on the other side of that rise. Coming closer, I could hear shouting, though I could see no one yet. Two voices I knew were screaming insults and threats.

"If you killed him, you're dead, you sick fuck!" came from Kurt, as he topped the rise and shot down the other side onto the access trail.

"I did, and I kill you too!" shouted Ulf, barely behind him and with something bulky in one bare hand, a ski pole dangling from his wrist.

Shit, well, obviously he hadn't, but the shot he fired at Kurt sounded damned sincere.

They didn't know I was there, and I hadn't a prayer of catching them as they hurtled toward the Cement Chute, but there had to be something I could do. I could handle the terrain, I told myself, it was just steeper than I was used to, and I knew what to do about steepness—cut across it at an angle. Turn to shed speed. Powder, well, I'd just have to not fall, because getting back up might be tricky. *Feet wider apart, like*

Jean-Claude Killy, Kurt's voice in my head suggested, and I sped down the access trail where only two skiers had gone before me.

The trail turned back into the trees, a large clump of scrubby pines to either side of an opening hiding the piste, but I could hear the shouting over the noise the mountain was making. Strange *whumpf* sounds, like a behemoth settling. Think about that later.

The trees would hide me from them, as well. Leaning into the downhill, I realized I'd been handed a weapon: surprise. Now if I could just aim it properly.

More shouting, this time from above. "Get off the slab! Get off the slab!"

Slab meant Mark—no time to think about it. I blew through the trees in time to see Kurt rise to his skis and lean down the forty degree slope. He became a red and black blur before Ulf could get up out of the churned snow where they'd scuffled, but he couldn't outski what Ulf pointed at him.

I came out of the trees, straight at Ulf, who fired again, the sound sharp against the groaning of the mountain. *Go, Kurt, go!* Ulf lined up his next shot, and I lined up mine.

I hit Ulf with my shoulder from behind, bringing him down with a grunt. The impact made me fight to keep my feet. The gun flew out of his hand. Blue steel nearly hit me as I cut back the other way in a flurry of speed and changed balance from the collision. Good, he'd have to hunt for it. Maybe I could get away fast enough that he couldn't bring me down with a bullet.

"Get off the slab!" Something hit me from behind. Only bent knees and sheer terror kept me upright. That and the arm around my waist—someone pulled me back into the trees.

"Keep going! Keep going!" Mark screamed at me. Branches

166

slapped at us—he dragged me between the pines. "We have to get as far uphill as we can!"

He let go, but kept going, fumbling with his equipment now. We used the momentum to get up the dished side of the slope, among trees that suddenly didn't look so sturdy. Something red whooshed and expanded, forming a huge, inflated ruff behind his head. Mark turned to me, arms open.

"Hang on to me!" was nearly lost in the mountain's roar. We grabbed each other in a world that went white and translucent.

The snow beneath us shook as the slab disintegrated, throwing spume into the air, blotting out the sun and sky in white needles. Unimaginable tons of snow flowed downhill. The snowpack gave way, drowning anything on it or in its path in white chaos. Crashing like surf, uncaring and inexorable, the avalanche roiled through the chute. Snow bashed against the mountain face on the opposite side of the slope, pulling trees away from our refuge.

Time stretched out in weird ways; the avalanche went on forever, but I could measure it with my breathing and Mark's as we pressed against one another. If the snow took us, holding onto him was my only hope of staying near the surface, and his emergency beacon would summon Marty even if we were buried. He was the only one who knew where I was, the only one who would have a clue where to search for my body. I held him literally for dear life. His warm breath against my neck was the only reminder that the slide hadn't taken us yet.

The roaring quieted as all that could tumble down the hill finished tumbling. Snow that had been thrown up fell back to the slope, and the sky was blue once more. The icy bedlam calmed. The mountain was only a mountain again.

"What do you know, we made it," Mark whispered against

my neck. He shoved his goggles down around his neck. They were caked in snow since he'd had to look out into the maelstrom while my own face was tucked into his neck and the inflated survival balloon. "Hurrah for being alive!" He took off my sunglasses.

At close range his straight brunet hair stuck out from under his cap in wisps, framing the warm hazel eyes that I hadn't seen clearly before. I cleaned the snow out of his eyebrows and wiped it from his cheeks. His wide mouth was almost too close to see, and then seeing didn't matter—he kissed me.

Hurrah for being alive, indeed. I opened my mouth and kissed him back, flooded with adrenaline and ecstasy at being upright and unburied.

It lasted three seconds—I yanked away, ashamed. "What about Kurt?"

"He had a big head start, Jake. I think he made it." Mark's face fell, though, knowing I was done with kisses for now and kisses with him forever. I let go of him and staggered back to the edge of the trees. I couldn't bear it if Kurt had not, if he'd been caught in the avalanche and lay suffocating while I kissed someone else.

"Ulf didn't." There was only blank snow where Ulf had been; the exposed under-layers that hadn't been strong enough to hold the weight of the last storms' leavings. I looked down the steep slope, looking for the blue and black clothing he'd worn, and in spite of Mark's assurances, for red and black, though I knew Kurt would have been much farther down the hill.

Mark pulled out his radio. "Snow Patrol Two to Snow Patrol One, do you read?"

"Son of a bitch, Mark, don't scare me like that!" Marty left all pretense of radio protocol behind in his relief.

"I'm all right, just have some snow down my neck. Jake is all right too," he reassured his partner. "We need to hunt for Ulf, though."

"Shit!" the radio crackled back. "Be right down. Did he have a beacon?"

Mark looked a question at me.

I shrugged. "Don't know about Ulf, but Kurt doesn't."

"Doubt it, but we'll listen." Mark touched something in his jacket that hummed and pulled a hidden valve that let the red bladder on his neck and shoulders deflate. "Never had to trigger the avalanche vest before." It settled in a plastic cape around him.

"We have to find Kurt!" I didn't know how to start, though Mark did. He pulled a long thin baton out of his belt and extended it into a pole.

"Sorry, Jake, but we know Ulf is in there, and we don't know if Kurt is. That guy is a fucking waste of space, but we're sure he was caught." Mark pleaded with me to understand, and I did, but I didn't, and I couldn't hope they found the guy who was doing his best to kill my Kurt. Punching Mark wouldn't change his mind.

Marty swung in. "He started from about here?" We nodded, all trace of elation gone. "Okay, we start from farther down, then." Marty looked sympathetically at me. "The guy in red was Kurt?" I nodded miserably. "Did you guys talk?"

I shook my head. "Not enough."

"Sorry, Jake. We have to look for that creep, but if you see anything, call your boss and tell him. He'll get on the radio and we'll come running with shovels, okay?"

"I can't. No phone." I was going to nail the damned phone to my ear just to make sure I always had it.

"Take the radio." Mark handed me something I didn't think he'd part with. "Call when you get to the bottom."

"Might take me a while." It might be longer than fifteen minutes, and some of that was gone already.

Marty looked concerned. "Can you get down this hill?"

I'd have to. "Yeah. Thanks, guys. I understand." As I swung down the hill after them, I wished I could scream and make them change their priorities, but one casualty was certain and one was only a possibility. I passed them sticking their probes into the snow.

Crisscrossing the narrow slope kept my speed down and gave me a wide sweep. The snow was lumpy and uneven, nothing like the groomed perfection of the slopes. I kept my eyes on the surface, picking my way as I searched for flashes of red, black, or equipment poking through the snow. I hoped I wouldn't overlook any trace of Kurt on my way down Cement Chute, but more than that, I hoped there would be no trace of Kurt in the snow here, that he'd gotten to safety. He had to have reached safety, though I dared not overlook anything, even through the tears.

TWENTY-TWO

The chute ended where the adjacent peak began and formed a huge dam for the snow. The avalanche had not made much of a turn, though the snow spilled out into the next track. I came down that steep section that hadn't existed until moments ago.

Nothing on Cement Chute said that Kurt was in the snow: no flash of red parka, no ski tip poking out, no shred of black pants. I'd searched as carefully as I could, knowing that the clock was ticking for a man buried alive, but nothing. Kurt had to have outrun the avalanche, he just had to have. I wiped my sleeve across my face and told myself that I'd found nothing of Kurt in the broken snow because he wasn't there to find.

Eighty miles an hour, Kurt had claimed for top flight ski racers and Mark had claimed for avalanches. "Kurt had a head start," I repeated aloud. "He had to have made it." But if I couldn't find him now, would I know before spring?

The trail here wasn't as steep. The snow was nearly unmarked; it hadn't been groomed and the powder was deep. The only flaw on the white snow was a black blit, just before the place where another ski run opened into this one. A couple of other skiers sailed out, making me wonder what they'd made of the avalanche. Had they even known that death had rumbled down the mountain? Would they care?

I looked ahead more than I looked down now, knowing that Kurt could not possibly be buried here, and the tears came down my face unheeded. So I nearly went past the black blit before I understood what I was seeing and why I could have been crying for joy since I got off the broken slab.

Idiot that I was, I hadn't registered that I was traveling through marked snow. Another trail marred the pristine powder here. It was hard to see in the noon light without much shadow, but it was there: another skier had been along this trail—only one, but there was only one it could be! Had he left me a sign?

The black thing was a glove! The snow near it was scuffed and marked, as if there was a message written in it, but the wind and the weight of the snow had rendered it illegible, even in the few short minutes since it had been written. Still, there was only one skier who could have left that trail, which came out from under the broken slab. I looked back to see, and yes, there were two trails, Kurt's and mine, behind me. The glove went into my pocket, and I kicked up to get going again.

I'd lost all my momentum when I'd stopped for the glove, so now I had to pole and swear to get back to the speed I'd had on this gentler slope that was access to the Lower Scott lift. Surely someone had seen a man with one glove come by—perhaps he was even still there, hoping to find me.

The lift was up ahead, and glory be, so was a figure in black and red, just outside the lift line, talking to someone. It didn't look like a happy conversation—Kurt waved his arms about and then grabbed the other person to shake him. One hand showed black at the end of his sleeve, one showed white and would be freezing cold. I couldn't hurry any faster, though

I poled harder when someone in a burgundy patrol jacket took his arm and tried to wrench him away. I had to get there before Kurt did anything that would get his lift ticket pulled, which a ski patrol could do for someone who made a disturbance.

As I got nearer, I could make out better what was going on.

"I have to get up there! Come on, Kim, please, you have to help!" Kurt was pleading and struggling now. Kim took him away from Gabe, who was patting him and telling him something I couldn't hear. Her brown curls bobbed with each shake of her head, making Kurt even more frantic. He grabbed her arm and begged, "Kim, you have to help me find him!"

I shifted my weight and screeched to a perfect parallel stop next to the little group, getting their attention at last. Pulling the glove out of my pocket, I offered it to Kurt, and everyone fell silent. "I think you dropped something."

I don't bring my immediate world to complete and total silence very often, but it was sweet to do it now. Gabe made goldfish mouths, Kim cocked her head, poodle style, and Kurt dropped his jaw. I twitched the glove at him, *come on, take it,* and he did, though I had to guide it into his hand. Mechanically, he put it on and found some composure again.

"That last run went okay, Jake?" he finally choked out.

"I'd have liked some warning about the bumps, but yeah." I could make this sound like something it wasn't.

"So everything is okay here?" Kim asked, and we all assured her that we were fine, fine, fine. The patrollers were the long arm of the law on the slopes, which made me wonder what Mark and Marty would have to say about our little adventure, but for now it was enough that she turned into the lift line and spoke into her radio. If Kim was going down Sundance, we'd be elsewhere.

"I don't suppose anyone wants to tell me what's going on?" Gabe asked plaintively.

"You mistake me for someone who knows what's going on," Kurt said, though he never took his eyes off me.

"Hey, I'm just out skiing." I shrugged. "Where next, Kurt?"

TWENTY-THREE

"Where next," Kurt repeated faintly, as if he couldn't believe that something so normal could be said on such a chaotic day.

"Yeah, do you want to do Prospector?" A narrow, thinly populated trail seemed like a really good idea, because then we could stop and talk with a bit of privacy, and I sure had things to say to him.

"No, I need to go up. I left my poles at the top." Now that he mentioned it, he looked strange, rather like the kids, with nothing in his hands.

"How did you do that?" asked Gabe, whose curiosity would be what killed the cat that got thrown across the icy driveway.

Relief must be making me delirious—I almost thought that made sense.

"Stuck them in the snow and skied off without them," Kurt told him offhandedly. I tossed my head toward the lift. Several people had come along already, so there was no chance of having to sit with Kim and dodge official questions.

"Well, duh," Gabe said for him. "Why did you do that?" The unofficial question asker was with us. Great.

"I was in a hurry." Kurt's tone said not to ask again. Gabe took the hint and headed to the lift with Kurt behind him.

I almost got to the rope barricade at the lift line before I got hit from behind. Must be my day for that, but this time the incoming was about waist height, dressed in pink, and bawling her head off. She might have been crying before we went down in a tangle of skis and poles, and only crying louder after, but it was hard to tell.

"Are you okay, Gracie?" I was concerned that she'd damaged herself and was too upset to notice. "Let's calm down, sweetie, whatever it is can't be that bad." We got ourselves somewhat organized, but before I could stand, she flung herself into my arms and sobbed into my neck. I sat back and let her cling, patting her gently and trying not to look at her father looming over me. It gave me a chance to grope around on the snow for my sunglasses.

"Maybe you can talk sense to her, Jake. She certainly isn't listening to me." The man who probably terrified ten businessmen before breakfast looked completely flummoxed by his kindergarten daughter. How was I supposed to do any better?

"Tell me what's the matter, honey." I suspected that black diamond runs were going to figure into this story somehow, and she did not disappoint.

"D-D-Daddy... said... no... black diamond slopes until I can p-pole plant!" she stammered out. "And I don't even have poles!"

"I don't think it's the poles, honey. I think it's the skills," I said, picking at the only part of this I understood, since I had no idea how to pole plant.

She wailed with the patent unfairness of this. "How am I gonna learn if I don't have poles?"

Oh no. She was attacking with kid logic. I met Mr. Underwood's eyes in horrified sympathy. He had to live with this every day.

I rubbed little circles on her back. "Gracie, I think you and your daddy have to talk about poles first, and then talk about learning to pole plant. But if you just cry at him, he's going to think you're too little for big kid things like poles." I petted her and willed her to calm down. From the corner of my eye, I could see Mr. Underwood nodding in agreement. I gave her a minute, which she used to control herself. The hiccupping stage was an improvement on the howling.

Kurt had come back to see what was keeping me; he opened his mouth to speak and shut it with a snap. He was wearing that sideways quirk that meant he was going to burst out laughing if I met his eyes, so I turned back to Gracie.

"But I want to go on Dynamite Alley todaaaaaaaaay!" still came out of her. "And Daddy said no!"

"Gracie, listen." I chose my words carefully. "Your daddy had to decide between making you happy and keeping you safe. He chose safe, even if it made you unhappy. And it was a good decision." I looked up at Kurt, who had gone solemn at my words, then back at Gracie. "Even if it made you really unhappy, and even if it made you mad. After you think about that for a while, you'll know that he made the right decision. Then you can stop being mad, and forgive him." I looked at Kurt again. His face was full of hope— I passed him a significant look before returning my eyes to her face. "Even if you don't know exactly why he decided that."

"Did you forgive Kurt?" she asked with the brutal directness of the very young.

"Yes." That was for Gracie. "Yes, I did." Now I looked up at Kurt. I had, from what little he'd been able to explain so far, and I told him so with my eyes. The rest would be only details. She followed my gaze.

"Could Kurt teach us to pole plant?" She looked up at me hopefully. Kurt nodded minutely.

"I think so, but he'd have to talk to your daddy first." Mr. Underwood flinched; it was all on his shoulders again. She followed my gaze, which had strayed back to Kurt, and scrambled out of my lap to cajole him, which she considered best done with arms around his waist. I lifted my poor cold butt up out of the snow.

"Please, Kurt? It would make Jake smile." If Kurt could resist that entreaty, he was a harder man than her father and a braver man than me.

"Ah! You must be the Kurt of whom I have heard so much." Mr. Underwood put out a hand. "You teach…?" Kurt took his hand gravely.

"Uh, I've parted ways with my last employer…." If Kurt wanted to throw Rudi under the bus, here was the perfect opportunity, but a death on this man's property, not to mention the man's marriage, was part of the stakes. Messengers were often shot. Kurt sidestepped that issue by saying, "I'd probably need to sign on with the Wapiti Creek Ski School."

"Do that. Talk to Charles Lewis." Mr. Underwood scribbled a note and a number on a card he'd pulled from a pocket. Golf courses and ski resorts, guess the only difference about the business transacted on them was the randomness of the encounters while skiing. "And be ready for a beginner/intermediate woman who had better damned well get up to speed after three years and a couple of five-year-olds who yearn to be Jorey Taylor."

"Ted Ligety, Daddy." Gracie grinned up at her father. "He skis prettier, and Jorey says Kurt can teach us to ski like that!"

"Oh, does he?" Mr. Underwood gave Kurt an appraising look. "Would you be Jorey's Shadow, by chance?"

"Once upon a time," Kurt said.

That made Gracie look at him oddly. "You're real, though."

"Yes," Kurt said. "Yes, I am."

When we loaded the Lower Scott quad lift, Gabe sat on Kurt's other side, effectively curtailing any chance of talking about the important things. He'd let others pass him by to find out more of what had just transpired, but Kurt and I weren't saying much, though we grinned goofily enough. I wanted to throw my arms around Kurt, to make him tell me what the hell had been going on, and make him promise never to do any of it again.

Gabe was just going to have to deal with public displays of affection. I slipped my arm into Kurt's and held it tight.

"Like that, huh," Gabe said knowingly. "Mark is going to be devastated."

"Mark already knows which way the wind blows," I responded, flinching a little at Gabe's knowledge, but done was done, and I wasn't letting go of Kurt for anything. I squeezed his arm a little tighter. He squeezed back, and I knew we'd need a long private time to finish what we'd just started.

"Does he? You're all he talks about," Gabe went on. I did not want to talk about Mark right now, maybe ever, because the taste of our kiss was still on my mouth. If anyone had some explaining to do, it was me.

"Sitting right here," Kurt said with some asperity.

"Yeah, well, it isn't as if an Alpenschlössl instructor should fuss about outside sweeties." Gabe had an overactive curiosity, an underactive tact gland, or a death wish.

Kurt just snarled at him. "I quit Alpenschlössl! Effective yesterday. I just need to get my hands on that miserable Rudi and get the paperwork straight. But I am not 'Alpenschlössl' anything! Got that?"

"Got it." Gabe shrank away from him. "But why did you sign on with them in the first place?"

Definitely a death wish, but Kurt must have seen the opportunity to clear his name, because he wouldn't release my arm so I could punch Gabe. "I was blinded by the bucks," Kurt went on more quietly. "I had no idea about the rest of it."

"You were the only one. That must have been a nasty shock." He must have decided Kurt's more reasonable tone meant he could keep probing.

"Oh yeah. But it didn't come to anything, except that Mrs. Walker grabbed my butt." Kurt shuddered. "And then I quit."

Gabe laughed, but I went cold inside. He'd been to the cabin. I trusted Kurt, I reminded myself, because he always had a good reason for what he did. If his good reason now was to get Gabe to spread the word of his innocence, I was all for it, even if it wasn't true. But, oh, how I wanted it to be true. I held his arm a little harder and swallowed down the lump in my throat.

At the top of the Lower Scott lift we had to unload and move to the second lift to go the rest of the way up the mountain. Gabe led the way, anxious to be back on station before his lunch hour was over. I trailed Kurt, who skated his skis to get some momentum without his poles. Halfway across the transit, a group of brightly dressed women spotted Kurt and surrounded him. I pulled up to avoid crashing into a cheerful woman with a rose-colored jacket and a nose full of pink zinc oxide, but when I heard what they were saying, I wished I'd hit her and taken the group down like dominos.

"Hey, Kurt, just in time! We were looking for you!" came from a tall woman in a silver jacket.

"Yeah, let's go back up to the cabin!" A woman in blue grabbed Kurt's arm. I could spear her with my pole from behind, but I'd let Kurt try to talk to her first.

"Your golden moment has passed, Cassie. We aren't going anywhere together." Kurt disengaged his arm, trying gently at first, but he got a little rougher as she clung.

"But you're my birthday present!" The clinger smiled coquettishly. "And him."

Oh hell no.

"Do we have to pay you more?" asked the woman in silver. I could spear her with the other pole.

"Yesterday I was bought and paid for, but the coin wasn't money. Today I am my own man. Let's go, Jake." He tried to escape the thicket of women, but was hampered without poles.

"We didn't even get your clothes off yesterday!" wailed Cassie. I wanted to cheer, but it was time to think instead. I'd seen the name Cassandra recently, on the list Kurt had abstracted from the Alpenschlössl computer. What did it go with? "You owe me!"

"No, I don't think so," I broke in, angry now. "It's Cassandra Rancier, isn't it?" They all swiveled around to stare at me, probably the same way they would if one of their little bug-eyed dogs had started to talk. I'd had to surf for information on this name, was it only the day before yesterday? "It's politicians that are supposed to stay bought. Want to talk about eminent domain?"

Kurt and I were abruptly alone. "How the hell did you do that?" he asked, bewildered.

I laughed deep in my chest. "You asked me to take a look at those names. Hers had a lovely scandal attached—properties getting condemned for proposed public works and then resold when the projects 'fell through.' Lots of juicy headlines."

"Knowledge is power." Kurt peered down the hill at the rapidly disappearing women. "Let's go get my poles."

TWENTY-FOUR

We had company up the hill, killing the opportunity for serious conversation once again. Only my thigh pressed against Kurt's kept me from losing the last shreds of control I owned. This had been the twenty-four hours from hell—more than anything else, I wanted some quiet refuge where I could be with Kurt.

"Getting home means getting down Killy's Knees," I pointed out. Blue/black runs were advanced intermediate. Everything else up there was black diamond or double diamond.

"Don't sweat it," Kurt said. "You've done harder already today, and you got my glove back."

This we could talk about even with a couple of teenaged snowboarders next to us. I didn't think Kurt was so distracted that he'd missed the significance of me getting on the Upper Scott lift, but he hadn't said anything. Since I wasn't going to let him out of my sight again, it wouldn't have mattered if he had.

"So don't worry." Kurt patted my leg and glowered when one of the teenagers snickered.

Somehow I didn't think that slow traverses on Cement Chute exactly qualified as "skiing a black diamond."

"Back to the scene of the crime," Kurt directed me, and I followed him down the access trail, herringboning my way up the rise. We looked down at the cabin, so innocently surrounded by snow and trees. One pair of skis and two sets of poles were stuck into the snow by the door. "Someone's there. I thought those were yours when I was here earlier, then things got a little busy."

"If he's waiting for Ulf, he could be waiting a long time. Mark and Marty are probably still looking. Oh yeah...." I'd been toting this radio around without using it. "Snow Patrol Two to Snow Patrol One, do you read?"

Kurt furrowed his forehead at me as I spoke into the unit.

"Snow Patrol One, over," crackled back at me.

"Skier in red jacket has been located in good condition. Over." No need to tell anyone who might be listening, like my buddy Egon, what was going on. Who knew how he spent all that time in the hut with the radio?

"Good. Over and out."

"Guess they aren't going to tell me about Ulf." I shoved the radio back into my pocket. "It's been a lot more than fifteen minutes since the slide."

"Did he get caught in that?" Kurt looked sick. "That's a horrible way to go."

"I'd feel worse if I hadn't watched him shoot at you." I pulled him against me with one arm. "Kurt, he wanted us both dead. I heard what he yelled at you." I kissed his cheek.

"You heard that?" He was stunned.

"I was coming along this very trail when you guys came over the rise, and I chased you into Cement Chute." The fear came back in a rush, because if Kurt had been shot and left on the slope, the avalanche would have hidden him until spring.

"I didn't know you were up there until I talked with Gabe. I left the glove for the patrols." He put his arms around my waist and his head on my shoulder. "I didn't see you."

"Neither did Ulf. I ran him over, and he dropped the gun in the snow." I kissed his head, but got a lipful of hat. Still, he was warm and alive; the snow hadn't touched him.

"Do you think he set off the avalanche? With the shot?" Kurt rubbed his cheek against me.

"Not likely. Mark said they use howitzers, and I know they planned to trigger. They probably had the cornice half sawed off when they saw people on the slope." I thought for a second—Kurt had patrolled in other seasons. "You know all that."

"I did, but I didn't know if you did. I don't want you blaming yourself for that sorry son of a bitch." He tipped his face, offering his mouth.

"I kept him from hurting you. The mountain took care of the rest." I took what he offered, treasuring the warmth and movement.

"Not the first time you've done that, Jake. You know, for a flatland 'furriner' city-boy, you have a pretty good understanding of frontier justice." He rubbed his nose against my cheek. "Let's go get my poles and tell the john he's out of luck."

The last time I'd kept someone from hurting Kurt, I'd shot at a knife-wielding biker with a bow and arrow. Missed him, but nailed his Harley, which might have been the more painful wound after all. Still, I'd meant to kill the guy, and I couldn't be too sorry that the snow and Ulf's own actions had done the job this time. If that was frontier justice, it suited me fine.

Kurt jammed his skis into the snow and strode to the glass door. He thumped on it, shouting, "Hello in there?"

"Where's Ulf?" asked the man who opened it. Fully dressed for the slopes, he could probably be mistaken for me if you didn't know either of us, being about my height, though older. I didn't sport either a cleft chin or a beer-belly, which was only too visible with just long johns on.

"Unavoidably detained. He won't be back up here today," Kurt told him.

"So they sent you instead? Very nice," he drawled, running his eyes over my Kurt. "Come on in."

"No. I'm not here for you." Kurt turned, but the man took his shoulder.

"You're Alpenschlössl and you're here. You must be." He tried to smile engagingly, but I'd had enough. I was out of my skis before he finished speaking, and jammed them upright into the snow.

"Buddy, your clothes are leaving the cabin in two minutes, and I don't care if you're wearing them or not." My ski boots rang loudly off the porch as I stomped to the door. Kurt had already disentangled himself, but I hadn't had one single adversary all day that I could square off with properly, and my nerves were completely shot. Someone was going to pay for bothering Kurt, and this guy looked handy. "And Kurt, take off the damned pin already."

"Uh, right." Kurt yanked off his gloves to pull the backing off the troublesome logo. I pushed through the sliding door. There had to be a bathroom in this little love nest.

I came out, drying my hands on a blue towel. "You're still here?"

The man stabbed into the recesses of his jacket, hunting for the second sleeve; it took several tries. Finally he grabbed his gloves, stammered, "Going!" and bolted. I glowered from the porch until he stumbled into his bindings and headed up the rise, his skis splayed widely as he herringboned up the hill and away from the madman. Kurt had come in and taken his boots and jacket off. Now he was sitting on the wooden bench by the fire, warming his gray-wool-clad toes.

I sat next to him, hunched forward with my forehead on my clasped hands. His hand was gentle on my back, rubbing lightly. "What do you want to do, Jake?"

"Can we just stay here a while?" It was quiet, it was warm, and there was no one else with me but Kurt. I did not want to look at any other human faces, speak any other names, hear any other voices. I needed the world to leave us alone.

"Sure. I thought that was why you threw the john out." He sat forward and drew my jacket off my shoulders, making me sway with the movement of my arms.

"It was that or hit him." I was so tired now that I wondered where I'd have gotten enough energy to hit the guy a second time if he'd resisted. All the adrenaline, anger, fear, and power that had kept me going all morning were gone, as if they had never been. I balanced my head carefully on my hands, because only the tripod effect would keep me upright. The fire was almost too warm on my face, but I couldn't really move away.

Kurt was rubbing my back again. His face looked the way I felt: he'd been through his own wringer today. Eyes closed, he asked the question that meant he wasn't going to listen to anything I said before I ate something. "Did you have any breakfast today, Jake?"

"There was cream in the coffee." I hadn't delayed following him to the slopes until my body had settled enough to feed it.

"Why do you do this to yourself?" he grumbled as he got up, returning with a wide mouth thermos and a spoon. Kurt pulled me upright against the back of the bench and sat close to me, holding the container below our chins. "Eat, okay?" The spoon brushed my lips, so I opened my mouth automatically, letting him tip vegetables and broth in. A spoonful went into his mouth while I chewed, then he fed me another. The soup disappeared into us, letting life and warmth return. I slipped a hand behind his head and stole a drop of broth that had escaped the corner of his mouth. He turned it into a tiny kiss and let me slide my cheek along his, even though my stubble rasped his smooth skin. He'd taken the time to shave this morning, though I had not, and the stroke raised the color in his skin. We'd been bright pink from the cold, which had faded to unfed pallor once in the cabin, but now he was uneven. I sanded his other side for symmetry, though he fended me off with the spoon.

"If you're this lively from the soup, I have great hopes for what the sandwiches will do to you." Kurt kissed me again before taking the empty container away and returning with bottles of water and a plate of deli excess, the sliced turkey mounded more than an inch deep in its nest of bread and mayonnaise. We each grabbed a triangle and gobbled in silence. Sighs of relief followed, which was my cue to take the plate back to the little table.

Sitting back next to Kurt, I brought up the six-hundred-pound gorilla. "Why was Ulf shooting?"

"I was going to go public about Alpenschlössl if Rudi didn't cut me loose. After yesterday, I don't think he or Ulf trusted me not to do it anyway. Jake, if he'd done even half of what he'd said he'd do to you, I'd have hurt them every way I could think of—publicity would have been just the start." He nibbled along my jaw, ending in a lopsided kiss.

I noticed anew that he had a puffy lip. "Did Ulf hit you?"

"No, Mark did, last night. Don't you remember?"

"Bits and pieces. It wasn't a good night."

"The Master of Understatement speaks. And you say that I jump to conclusions." Kurt pulled me back against his arm. "Though your conclusions weren't entirely out there."

"The women made it pretty plain that it didn't go the way they expected." I rested a hand on his thigh.

"For which the good Lord, you, and Renzetti's Pizza are to be thanked. She threw me out after a visitation from the Ghost of Garlic Past." Kurt chuckled at the memory.

"The Ghost, oh…." I wanted to laugh. If he'd told me this before I'd eaten, I might have cried instead. I swung my arm behind his head and brought his face to mine. "I don't scare so easily." Mindful of the damage, I slipped my tongue along his lower lip, meeting his tongue in the softest of caresses. "And neither do you. What did Ulf say?"

He looked straight ahead, into some future that wouldn't happen now. "Jake, what he threatened makes me hope the avalanche finished him, just so he can't ever touch you. I'd have done whatever I had to, yesterday, to keep him from shooting to maim. Or—" He stopped; the pain in his face said enough. "And I did, I fixed it, but Jake, I really hope he's dead."

"If he touches either one of us, he is for sure," I told him, and then it was time for both of us to quit talking.

TWENTY-FIVE

It would be easier to get the ski pants off if I took the boots off first. We stood up to strip each other and were doing pretty well until we got to my pants.

Kurt pushed me back onto the bench and then took one boot off with a mighty heave, while I tried not to slide off the seat. Then he wrenched the other one off and slipped the long johns and ski pants the rest of the way down my legs while he was at it, throwing them on the floor behind us. We still had two pairs of socks each, but they weren't in the way.

Noticeable, though. He looked down at my one gray wooly foot and one white wooly foot. I'd bought a different color so we could keep the laundry straight. "Oh, Jake." He knelt between my knees and ran his hands up and down my legs as he chuckled over my comfort clothing.

"I missed you this morning." I pulled him against my chest; we were skin to skin now, with the gas log casting warmth. His buns were aimed toward the fire. Their lightly toasting surfaces were warm under my hands.

"I missed you last night," he said. "That bed is too empty without you."

If I'd taken Mark up on his offer, one thing I did recall a little too well, this conversation might be going a very different direction. "There's a bed over there, calling our names."

What were we waiting for? Our sock feet had no traction on the dash across a few yards of wood flooring, but we did manage to make it to our target.

After months of camp cots and sleeping bags in the cabin and sex on any handy boulder, fallen tree, or meadow, it was still strange to slide into a bed. The sheets were as crisp as they looked, cool against my skin. The turned-down comforter came to my waist, covering my erection, but the air was much chillier here in the corner of the cabin, so I flipped the goose-down up over our shoulders. Turning to face Kurt, I marveled at how his tanned, blond good looks showed against the white pillows. His chest was bare and exposed to my hands, if not my eyes, so I stroked his skin. His hard cock was concealed but not imprisoned. I needed only to slide my hand farther to find his erection.

Knowing he was hidden but accessible excited me—our alfresco sex had left me unaware of how tantalizing a little bedding could be. I explored his exposed skin first, kissing and licking my way across his neck, then ducking down to his chest. He ran strong hands down my back, massaging and investigating. Moans rumbled from his throat, and then I had to come up to catch the sounds in my mouth. I lay on top of him now, skin to bare skin, the covers still hiding our bodies. He sought my lips as eagerly as I sought his, the puffiness making the kiss awkward. We laughed a little when our teeth clinked together.

"Easy, Jake," he said, licking my lower lip, but he didn't stop the sensuous motions of his hips as our hard cocks rubbed together, trapped between our bellies. He felt so good, so right, pressed to my flesh. If we were any closer, one of us would be inside the other, and I could barely wait for that. He nibbled my neck, taking skin between his teeth, softly nipping, making me shiver. "Cold?" he teased, but no, I was hot for him, and he knew it.

I repaid the favor by sucking his earlobe into my mouth. Hot breath and tiny licks there could reduce him to quivering, and I loved to do it to him. He moaned as I traced the rim of his ear with my tongue, and he began to massage the base of my spine on either side, which shot strange sparks through me and caused me to cry out.

He stopped, because we'd learned that a little of that went a long way, and started to work his fingers into my back again, traveling up my spine. "Oh, that is good," I mumbled into his neck, as I slipped my hands up under his shoulders to do the same to him. With hands, mouths, and bodies, we kneaded each other in the light from the windows and the flickering gas log.

Wondering if Kurt thought this concealment was as exciting as I did, I started wiggling my way down to the foot of the bed, pulling the covers over my head. I had to be a lump in the bedclothes crouching over his groin, taking his hard cock into my hand. Stroking him from the base up let me feel his excitement; seven inches of hardness was mine to play with, and I did, slipping his skin over his shaft. A tiny bit of light filtered through the sheet and the down, letting me see what I was about to put into my mouth.

The covers did nothing to muffle his panting and exclamations, which grew louder as I sucked his balls into my mouth one at a time, letting them slide out again and nibbling the rough, slightly furry skin of his sack.

"Have some mercy under there, Jake," he gasped. He thrust a hand beneath the covers to stroke my hair. I'd let mine grow out more too, and it was making curls at the back of my neck, which he played with at times like this.

"Nevah!" I growled playfully, and sucked the tip of his cock, with its little bead of moisture, into my mouth. I took more and more of him in, swirling my tongue over the soft head, down the hard shaft, before coming up again. Intending to do this to him until he ended with orgasm, I set about sucking Kurt into a frenzy. Not being able to see his face was a good thing this once, since he might have distracted me from my single-minded application of mouth to cock.

I had to slip one hand under his thigh to catch his wrist before he could change my rhythm, and when he put his other hand under the covers, I caught that wrist too. Nothing would suit me today other than Kurt spending himself into my mouth as I played with him from my hiding place. Imagining what he was seeing, a bouncing white lump under the duvet, while feeling my familiar tonguing, made me even harder than before, so when he wiggled a foot under me and rubbed his leg against my cock, I rubbed back and redoubled my efforts with my mouth.

Finally, I had to release his wrists to hold his shaft with one hand and his balls with the other, plunging my mouth over his cock. He curled around my head enough to grab my shoulders. The pleasure overwhelmed him, and I heard his strangled cry as he pulsed and came. For long seconds he throbbed and spurted, giving me what I wanted, before falling back against the pillow to catch his breath.

He gasped, and I uncurled, easing my way back into the fresh air and the light, finally stretching out full length against him, the covers drawn up to our armpits. My hard cock pressed against his side. I'd just give him a few moments to get ready for whatever we did next. When he had enough breath to kiss me, it would be time enough to move on, and in the meantime, I could caress his arms and sides.

"What you do to me, Jake," he murmured, as he sought my mouth with his. I'd been completely inexperienced when he first took me, but I'd learned a lot these last five months, and I loved being able to please him.

"What else shall I do to you?" I asked, knowing his orgasm might influence his opinion of what he wanted now.

"I think you'll give me the chance to return the favor," he said between kisses, and then plumped the pillows behind his head. "Come up here where I can suck you."

I'd never turn down that offer from him—it was the first sex he'd ever proposed to me, and it never grew old to feel his mouth on my cock, though today some caution was in order. "Even with the fat lip?"

"Just get up here!"

Eagerly I escaped from under the comforter to straddle his shoulders, letting my cock wave enticingly near his mouth. I'd have to be careful, since his hands were behind me and he couldn't control the depth, but he'd grown steadily more skilled at taking my eight inches down to the base. With his hands on my hips, Kurt guided me to his lips, licking me all over as my cock jumped away from his tongue. Part of it was me shivering, because the head of the bed was away from the fire.

"What idiot made this bed?" Yanking the goose-down untucked and throwing the pillows toward Kurt's feet, I turned us around so my bare body was in the warm zone. The brass bed frame was lower at this end, but no matter, Kurt was warm under the comforter and now so was I, over his head.

"A little help here," he said with his tongue out and waving.

My cock came down to bat his nose when I swung my leg over him again. He licked me again as I used a hand to aim my cock into his mouth, and then he let his lips slide along the length of my shaft.

Grabbing the footboard with both hands to steady myself, I thrust gently into his mouth. Grateful for the stability, I looked down at the wonderful sight of my cock disappearing between his lips, feeling his tongue stroke me into pleasure that once I'd only imagined with him. Kurt set the speed, moving my hips with his hands, and I moaned his name as his eyes fluttered shut.

With one especially sensuous swirl, he let go of my cock and craned upward to his hand, which he was straining to get around my thigh and into his mouth. One strong finger got sucked to wetness in two long strokes, and then he was trying to catch my cock again, so I lifted my butt to help. That must have been the rest of the help he needed too, because it parted my cheeks just enough for him to find my asshole, to slip that wet finger in.

He fingerfucked me gently as I fucked his mouth now; feeling these two connections with him made me throw my head back. I slid in and out of him, he slid in and out of me, and my knuckles were white as I squeezed the footboard. When he pressed down on that great spot and increased the pressure of his lips, it tipped me over the edge to climax, filling this little cabin on the mountaintop with a sound made only by the mountain lions and me.

Once I could move again, I lay down beside him, head on his shoulder. I held him tightly, thinking that this would be a great time to tell him how much I loved him, and then kept quiet. I didn't want Kurt to think I only meant the sex was great, or that I was glad we were good with each other again.

Too much else had happened today that would contaminate the words.

He tucked up the covers around me, stroking my shoulder and kissing my hair. "Are you my happy man again?" he asked me, and the hope in his voice was a palpable thing.

"Very happy and very yours." I could tell him that without the baggage of the other words, and I held him even more tightly.

"Good," he murmured. "I... I think we have time for a nap."

TWENTY-SIX

Nature woke me, though she'd let me sleep just long enough to be refreshed. I eased out of the bed without waking Kurt, stopping to brush a lock of hair off his forehead. His lashes lay against his cheeks, long and sandy blond like his brows. The swollen lower lip disturbed his handsome symmetry, leaving his lips parted on the one side only. We'd taken a lot of risks with each other and for each other, but this was the first physical marking he'd taken on my account. He'd wished Ulf dead, though, so the psychological marks had gone deep. When I got back, I'd spoon him from behind, to protect him from whatever I could.

It might have been his empty arms that roused him and sent him in search of me, but he found me in the tiny bathroom, unwrapping one of the miniature toothbrushes at the side of the sink. He rubbed one eye while he watched me generate a mouthful of foam, before standing with his back to me at the familiar fixture of the two.

"What's that thing?" I asked, after I'd rinsed my mouth. Twisting a knob shot a fountain of water into the air. I turned it off a lot faster than I'd turned it on, even though the basin caught the water.

"It's a bidet. They're all over in Europe." Kurt started brushing his teeth with another tiny toothbrush. "Makes sense —" He stopped to rinse. "—to have one up here."

"Why?" I regarded the rimless basin with the spigot, knobs, and drain with some suspicion.

"Because it's not for washing socks, which is what I did the first time I found one." Kurt chuckled. "This is a sex hideaway, and it's for washing you."

"The sock thing is a little more obvious," I started to say, but Kurt steered me until I was straddling the basin, then sitting down, with my tackle dangling in. "Uh… oh!"

He turned the knobs, shielding me from the water until he'd gotten the temperature to his satisfaction, and then taking his hand away to let the fountain hit me right in the nads. The warm water felt good, if strange, and then Kurt knelt beside me, one arm around my waist. He pumped a bit of soap into his hand. "The whole point is to spot clean your crotch," he told me as he rubbed the soap all over my cock and balls, "any time you'd like." He paused to kiss me. "Europeans think we're a bunch of barbarians for relying on toilet paper alone. Scoot up."

Moving farther onto the bidet as he patted my butt, I could see the point. This was deluxe and got better. He took another pump from the soap dispenser before Kurt sliding his hand into my crack, working suds into every little crevice. He slipped against my asshole, and I understood exactly why he said, "If we ever have a bathroom to build or remodel, we're putting in one of these."

"Oh yeah." I'd already put my arm over his shoulders, to encourage his kisses, but now I needed him for balance as he teased me with a soapy finger. My cock was already coming back up, and I was getting anxious for him to slip that teasing finger into me. "Get me really clean."

"Plan to." He finally penetrated my ass, stealing my reason with his soft pumping. "And really rinsed too, or I'm going to be hiccupping bubbles."

It took me a second to figure that one out, and then I nearly fell off the bidet.

"Yeah, Jake," he whispered into my mouth as he let the water gush over me. "I'm gonna taste."

Pretending to myself that my wobbly knees were from all that hard skiing and not from anticipation let me get to the bed without actually falling, though when Kurt tipped me onto my back, it was just barely in time. He tucked the goose-down around us as we shivered slightly from the chill air. The gas fire didn't warm as far as the bathroom.

"You aren't going to stop me like you did that once, are you?" Kurt rolled on top of me, tracing my features with his fingertips.

"That was before I met the bidet. Though I might—" I kissed the fingertips dancing lightly over my lips. "—start screaming something about 'Fuck me now'!"

"I'll fuck you when we're both good and ready," he promised, blue eyes dancing. "And I'll be the judge of when."

Take your time, I thought, as we rolled together, kissing and nibbling. An afternoon in bed was new for us, though we'd had our lazy afternoons by the lake and in the woods. The bed was soft and springy, with no stray pinecones or sharp rocks to find the hard way, and if the temperature was cooler on one end, we could just hide in the down comforter. I found myself on top of Kurt, licking him between the shoulder blades and running my hand down his flank, planning to grab a handful of ass. When he flinched, I stopped.

"What's the matter?" Rising over him, I looked down to see what I'd done.

"Nothing. Get back down here." Kurt stuck a hand between my thighs to pull me close.

"This is a big honking bruise, Kurt, not 'nothing'." I sat back on my heels to take a better look at the black and blue comet across his flank, just above his waist. None of the adventures I knew about so far accounted for damage that flared backward from a nasty, dark-centered blotch. "What happened?"

"Egon stabbed me with his pole this morning. Seems he wants my job." Kurt rolled to his back and yanked me down on top of him again.

I leaned down to kiss the bruise. "He can have it."

Our play eventually put me on the bottom on my belly in the warm zone at the foot of the bed with Kurt lying on top of me. His cock was nestled into my crack, his lips near my ear, and his hands slipped under my shoulders. On any other day, I'd have lifted my ass to slide him in, but now I lay still. Catching one of his fingers in my mouth, I licked it softly, wanting him to feel my urging, yet not wanting to pressure him.

"You are so amazingly sexy," he whispered between nibbles on my neck, then sat up. "I can hardly stand it."

Me? Uh, okay, I wouldn't argue with him, especially since he was straddling my back now, his hands flat to my skin, and scooting backward a few inches at a time. When his butt was on top of mine, he leaned down to lick a line across my spine, then resumed his slow travel backward.

He had my thighs trapped under him now, his hands on my buttocks. Squeezing, playing, kneading, it was all sweet torment and anticipation for what I hoped he hadn't changed his mind about. When he parted my cheeks, he moaned, and I knew I'd just have to hang on a little bit longer. I helped him play with my ass, little hip thrusts pushed my buns into his hands, rubbing my cock, hard and leaking, against the bedding below.

Small noises came out of me from the way Kurt was working his fingers into the muscles of my butt, in time with the motions of my hips and his, rubbing his ass against the backs of my knees. Then he wasn't there anymore—he was on his knees. One strong hand pressed down on my upper back, and the other slipped under my hips to raise them. Following his silent directions, I put my ass in the air for him.

Seeing what he did when we had sex was really important to me. I liked the positions where I could see his face, his body, or both, and butt up didn't work well for me that way. If he was going to reach, though, I'd just have to deal with it. Crushing a pillow to my chest gave me something to hold as he put his face down and nipped softly at one cheek.

"Ohhhh…." He drew the tip of his tongue across my cheek and breathed softly into my crack. He'd arrived high and now licked his way down to more sensitive places, reaching my hole after wonderful, excruciatingly long seconds. Little flicks and longer licks made me moan again, loving the way Kurt tongued me there, where he'd been the first and only one to enter. Now he played me with his mouth, the sensuous swirling of his tongue giving way to little nibbles on my cheeks when he came up for air. I was so open to him as he spread me wider with his hands to plunge his face into my crack.

Seeing what he was doing was impossible; feeling what he was doing was my whole world right then. I had to bite the corner of the pillow to keep from screaming. To hell with it, he should know that he was driving me wild—the pillowcase tore in my teeth when I pulled away.

His name was the only word in my cries, but, "Ahhhhhhhh, Kurt!" brought him back from nibbling a bun and teasing me with a finger to mouthing my ass more intimately. He took his tongue back long enough to say my name softly and then stroked it across my hole again.

Is this what I'd done to him the other night, when I'd folded him like origami on the couch? Had I driven his thoughts away, the way mine were going, chased by his tongue? He reached under me and had a handful of cock now, not stroking, just holding me and letting my own movements fuck his hand. Kurt had me every way he could like this, and I could only call his name again to say how good it was.

"Oh, man, you are hot stuff, Hot Stuff." Kurt swiped his tongue across my hole, making the muscle relax under his attentions. "Damn."

Damn, yeah. As he probed my ass, I thought about screaming now, begging him to fuck me, but that would mean leaving off the licking and lapping. But damn, I wanted his cock in there, and I wanted it now. If he didn't have to stop. Damn. "Kurt…." I managed to gasp out.

"Yeah?" He lifted his mouth away from me enough to respond, then put it back.

"Now?" My voice wasn't working any better than that. "Fuck" was too hard to say.

"Soon." Now he had both hands on my ass and his mouth right… there.

And then, not. He'd grabbed something, and while his tongue caressed me, his hands were elsewhere. His warm mouth disappeared, making me whimper, and then something chilly hit my crack. I yipped and rose off the pillow, but he pushed me back down, soothing me, saying, "It's okay, Jake, it will be warm in a second," and stroking his fingers through the goop and into me to make it so.

Now, it had to be now, and it was, as Kurt penetrated my very relaxed ass with his hard cock and bore me down to the mattress. "Told you I'd fuck you," he whispered into my ear, "when you're good and ready." He slipped farther into my ass, spreading his legs to match mine. His chest was flat to my back, his thighs pressed against mine, and his hands gripped my upper arms. "Oh, you are ready." I could see him as I turned my head almost farther than it would go, just his face, as he plunged deeply into me.

Deeply and slowly he took me, as if relearning the way. Perhaps the boundaries had changed the way terrain changed after an avalanche, but all I knew as I rose to meet his hips was that my lover wanted to touch me in every possible way, and that I wanted him to do it more than I'd ever wanted him before. Damn the position for not letting our mouths meet, but I would kiss him again after, and now, he stretched every movement out to fuck me. The sweet, slow strokes and his skin against mine counteracted every rotten thing that had happened all day.

Kurt's ragged breath was hot on my neck. He pumped faster the closer he came to climax. Matching him risked him slipping out. It was far too wonderful to chance, so I held still as he thrust into my ass, welcoming the stretch and pounding inside as he grew wilder. For leverage, he finally had to raise himself above me on his hands, to plunge into my ass with crazy, desperate speed.

He exploded into me with a strangled cry, pulsing and throbbing with his orgasm. I could barely breathe from his weight falling against me. I'd have to outwait his pleasure to get my face out of the pillow. We could both breathe again after a while, then he let me turn over and rested his face against my chest. I held him, happy to have found him again, happy to hold him, willing to wait for my own release until he could share it with me.

"Hey, Hot Stuff." Kurt lifted himself high enough to kiss me. Sweet and slow again, we brushed against one another, tongues sliding softly. Lipping the puffy part of his mouth as gently as I could, I told him without words that I was sorry he'd gotten hurt on my account, but that I'd heal him, kiss him better, love him to wellness again, and he nibbled back, before stroking his cheek against my stubble. His hand stole to my groin, where my erection swelled, hard and hot in his palm.

Matching the speed of his hand to the speed of his tongue, Kurt kissed and stroked me, swallowing all my incoherent sounds. I couldn't stay still against him. My hand behind his back strayed from waist to butt, groping and caressing. With my other hand, I controlled the kiss, slipping my fingers through the curls at the back of his neck, begging him for more of everything he could do.

When my climax hit, I hid my face in his neck, clutching his ass and spattering my chest with hot fluid. My cock jumped in his hand as he coaxed the last spasms out of me, making the droplets of come land on my skin. The tremors dwindled and faded away after a time, but I couldn't let Kurt go now that he was in my arms once more. He gazed down at me, and I knew all was right with my world again: his dimple was showing.

TWENTY-SEVEN

I could have stayed in bed for hours yet, but there was a small matter of getting off the mountain in daylight.

"Rudi's supposed to meet me." Kurt got up to find his clothing. "I am going to get this straightened out once and for all, and I want to do it before he finds out about Ulf." He still had his socks on, which would save him a good five minutes of hunting runaways.

"We haven't found out about Ulf." Not that I had a lot of hope for him; the avalanche had been more relentless even than fire.

"We will. You still have that radio." Kurt lifted the bib straps over his shoulders.

Poking my head out of the fleece, I had to agree. "I need to give it back. Mark would probably be in trouble for giving it to me."

"He would. Bet that won't figure in his report." Kurt turned off a valve, making the flames wink out on the gas log.

Bet a lot of things wouldn't figure in his report. For that matter, I hadn't reported quite everything to Kurt about Mark.

The guilt nipped at me, but it was a kiss, broken off and never to repeat, so first things first. With consternation, I watched Kurt lock the cabin door.

"I'd throw this into the snow, but I'd rather shove it up Rudi's ass." Kurt stuck the key in his pocket. "Especially if Ulf was acting on his instructions. He threatened to kill me yesterday, so it's kind of hard to tell." He gave me a quick kiss before he dropped his skis on the snow to step into them.

"He did?" Again I was grateful to the mountain for taking care of the threat to my lover.

"He didn't like all the suggestions I was making. Come on." Kurt looped the straps over his wrists and dug the poles into the snow. "Killy's Knees ahead!"

I followed him up the rise and down, and then a little farther up, before arriving at the top of the run. The sign had a blue square with a black diamond in it, telling me there was a greater challenge here than I'd faced before.

"Ready?" Kurt grinned at me. I grinned back. After everything else that happened today, what was a blue/black hill to worry about?

"Ready!" I poled over the brink and headed down the slope.

Speed? I laughed at speed, picking up more on my way nearly straight down the top of the trail. I didn't try to turn in the fluffy churned powder and barely turned once I came to the more heavily groomed snow. "Whooo!" I yelled, sliding around a curve, shooting past a surprised woman who was helping her companion up off the snow.

"Whooo!" Kurt yelled from behind me, telling me he was pacing me and enjoying it. "Shred it, Jake!"

Whatever, I was having a blast sailing down that hill, which had widened out after the curve. The snow was mine as I shifted my weight, carving long curves down the hill, reveling in the steepness and the speed. The bumps at the bottom did inspire me to a little caution—Kurt and I hadn't done moguls yet. Someone was pounding his way through the mogul field, though I could devote little attention to how he bounced from one mound to the next in the long section. The sides tapered to only a few bumps.

"I'm gonna do it!" I yelled to Kurt and the world. If I went slightly to the right and popped to the left, right... *now!* My skis sprang from one hillock to the second—I flexed again and ran out of bumps just in time. Coming out of the moguls flailing, still I kept my feet, which made me scream my triumph through to the end of my skidding stop.

"Wahoo!"

"Yaaaahh!" Kurt hit the mogul field at its deepest point. I watched him blast through about nine hills before coming back to even snow. His upper body barely moved as he bounded through. From the waist down he was a spring. His feet moved with a life of their own, dancing from mogul to mogul.

"Wahoo!" I yelled again, shaking my poles at the sky, amazed by what he could do. "Dayum!"

"Wahoo!" he screamed back, pumping his fist. "That was great!" We clanked our poles together in an overhead salute before turning down the hill again.

The radio crackled before we reached the lift. I'd nearly forgotten it in the joy of the run. Now I was called back to reality.

"Snow Patrol One to Snow Patrol Two, over."

I cranked to a halt to fumble the radio out of my pocket. Yanking a glove off, I found the push-to-talk button. Kurt pulled up in time to hear me respond, "Come in, Snow Patrol One."

"What is your location?" I looked at Kurt, who looked back

with concern. Marty's voice was crisp and businesslike, no trace of elation. That couldn't be good.

"Killy's Knees, just above the junction."

"Get to the junction and wait. Out."

More slowly now, we skied to the junction with the black diamond run, choosing to wait inconspicuously at the uphill side of Killy's Knees, where no one had reason to look for us. Other skiers drifted past as we waited, mostly off Killy's Knees, but patrollers in burgundy jackets whipped past us off Cement Chute. I slipped my arm into Kurt's, needing some kind of contact, but neither of us broke the silence.

Waiting for bad news made the time pass slowly, but eventually two more skiers in burgundy jackets appeared above us, turning to come down off the slab at the shallowest angle possible. The stretcher Mark pulled might have flipped had he taken a more aggressive approach. Marty skied behind the toboggan holding the stabilizer bar, and the set of their shoulders said everything about what they'd had to do since the slide.

"We found him," Marty said, when they pulled up next to us, hidden from the blue/black slope by the trees. "It took us and the other six guys close to two hours just to find him." He sniffed hard. "Might have gone faster if we'd had the dogs, but they're up at Telluride. There was a backcountry slide yesterday, and they're still hunting."

"Wouldn't have mattered." Mark swiped an arm across his face. "His neck was broken, maybe his spine farther down too."

"Then it was fast?" I couldn't grieve for Ulf, but I couldn't wish him a lingering death either. I glanced at the stretcher, where a black tarp covered the body head to toe.

"Lord, I hope so," Mark said. "It could have been one of us." He turned from me to Kurt and looked down at the snow.

Marty was closest. He put an arm over Mark's shoulder on top of the deflated avalanche balloon. "Or all of us."

"But it wasn't. Because of you guys." Kurt stepped forward and touched Mark's arm. "I heard you yelling and got the hell out of there. Thanks."

"You dragged me off the slab." I put my hand over Mark's where he held the stretcher handle. "So thanks." I'd tell Kurt the rest of it later.

"I didn't even try for Ulf," Mark said brokenly. "I saw him shooting. I saw Jake knock him down. He tried to catch the gun before he fell." Mark looked around at us, his face begging for understanding. "He was trying to kill you. I didn't even think to grab him...."

"Mark, you saved the good guys." Marty shook him just a little. "He was down, still trying to kill them. You did right." More softly, "You did right. Even though you shouldn't have gone onto the slab at all."

"I couldn't not...." Mark looked at me. "I had to...."

Kurt stepped up against him, skis parallel. "I'm glad you did, Mark. Thank you." He put his arms around Mark, who trembled against Marty. A strange echo shook me—Mark had comforted Kurt, was it only last night? Kurt lifted his lips to Mark's ear and whispered something I couldn't hear, but it made Mark slump in their arms and my heart slump for him.

I slipped up on the high side of Marty's skis and added my own arms to the embrace. Both Marty and Mark had had to clean up the mess that we'd been part of. I couldn't imagine shoveling snow away to reveal a corpse, even if I'd hated and feared the man in life. "I'm sorry you guys had to do this," I told them, and met Kurt's eyes. They were so full of pain. How could we make this any better?

"I've never dug out a dead one," Mark said against Kurt's

shoulder. "In four years, I've never had to recover a body, let alone someone I knew. Even if he was a total shit." I could barely reach his arm, but I patted it forlornly.

Marty looked up at me, a tear running out from under his sunglasses. I squeezed him a little harder. "Mark, we've got to get it together, we need to get down. They're waiting for us."

Mark hesitated on letting go when I needed my hand back to extract the radio from my pocket. "Here. I won't mention that I had it."

His laugh had no mirth. "You didn't have it. You never had it. You don't know what happened, and you weren't anywhere near." He shoved it into his pocket, and it may as well have been there all day.

"He's right, you know." Marty sniffed again. "If we tell your part in this, Jake loses his job. You both lose your lift tickets. You're screwed and it doesn't touch Ulf—he's dead. So, we have no idea why Ulf was out on Cement Chute shooting at a couple of strangers when it was closed, and you guys were over on the East Peak. Anywhere but here. We haven't seen you all day."

Mark pulled away from everyone, leaning away from Kurt and shaking off Marty. He dropped the stretcher handle, pulling out from under my hand. With a lean of his head, he moved Kurt backward to escape through the opening with the stretcher chasing him.

"Yeah. It never happened." Mark looked back at me, his face drawn. "And you were never there."

TWENTY-EIGHT

We watched them ski away, pulling their grievous burden. Ulf had paid the stakes he was trying to extract from others, but men who had no part of his scheme would pay too. I had to touch Kurt.

"Better Ulf than you," I whispered. "I'm just sorry they got caught up in it all."

"Me too, and you know what? This absolutely screws over what I'd planned to do to Rudi. If I throw him under the bus, they go too. I can't do that." Kurt furrowed his brow. "I was just going to turn it all over to the media and James Underwood, but they'll get fired for trying to protect us. Shit."

"Any idea for Plan B?" I asked. Glumly considering the possibilities, I couldn't see any course that punished only the deserving. Someone was going to end up happier than he had a right to.

"Yes, as a matter of fact, I do. Or rather, you did. Come on, we need Egon!" Kurt kicked down the trail after the patrols, who bypassed the lifts, heading instead to the patrol hut where an ambulance waited without lights or sirens.

The bunny lift was going to close soon. We'd spent the entire afternoon on the mountain. What could we need that self-centered cretin for? Kurt had a plan; resolution stiffened his spine. "Hey, Egon!" Come here!" he yelled once we got there. "Lift's closing, people. The day is over now," he told the skiers who tried for one last run, and blocked the rope lanes. "Good night, good night," he said, turning them away. "The lift operators need to shut down, hope you had a good day!" He kept this up until the last passengers offloaded at the top and the lift stopped.

"Oh, you are boss of the mountain now, Alpenschlössl?" Egon strode down from the hut.

Kurt reached into his pocket. "I'm not Alpenschlössl, you are." He handed over the pin. "I'm out of there; they need an instructor. Come on, let's go tell Rudi."

We skied slowly on the flat. Egon in polar boots had no trouble keeping up with us. "This after I nearly kill you?"

I'd seen the bruise, but what the hell had I missed?

"You weren't even close, pal, and you should be grateful for it." Kurt paused to get out of his bindings. We'd make better time carrying our skis on the flat. Poking my pole into the bindings, I followed suit.

"Then why do you do this for me?" Egon was puzzled and so was I.

"Because you understand exactly what they want, and you don't mind. The job sucks, you suck, and you deserve each other. Don't know what you think, Egon, but I don't see this as doing you a favor, even if you want it." Kurt marched toward the Alpenschlössl office, skis over his shoulder. "I'm doing it for other reasons completely."

We stuck our skis into the snow by the door. "You go in first, Egon, and talk loud enough that he knows it's you," Kurt told him and put a hand on my arm to keep me back. "He won't be happy with me right now, but he'll do things my way."

"Okay." Egon clomped up the stairs and through the door. "Ho, Rudi! Rudi Gernsbach! Egon Bachov here! You there?" We paused in the doorway.

"Is Carlson with you?" floated out through the door.

"You listen to him, Rudi, we all be happy, okay?" Egon looked back at us, concerned. "I have Carlson and Landon too. We talk, okay?"

Movement showed over Egon's shoulder. "Put gun down, Rudi!"

"Dead man switch! Dead man switch!" Kurt screamed over Egon's shoulder, as the big Bulgarian tried to back out the door. Couldn't blame him. Whoring was one thing, but getting shot at was another.

"*Scheiße!*" Rudi swore, and something clattered on wood. "Come in. I won't hurt you. What the fuck do you mean, 'dead man switch'?"

"Hands empty," Egon whispered over his shoulder, and went the rest of the way into the office. We followed gingerly, ready to pounce. Rudi, clad in gray fleece and black stretch ski pants, stood in the doorway between the main room and his office.

"Your buddy Ulf nearly fucked you over today," Kurt told his ex-boss. "If he'd shot me this afternoon, you'd have been in a world of hurt." Kurt stood tall and strong, confident in what he was saying. "The *Denver Post*, four television channels, and *Time Magazine* would have been fighting over your client list, while James Underwood hunted Ulf's ass, and yours, off the continent. Is that what you want?"

"Certainly not!" Rudi blazed.

"Then you want me healthy, happy, and away from you.

Especially happy. Especially away from you. Especially healthy. Jake here too." Kurt stood toe to toe with Rudi, who seemed to shrink in on himself. "I quit—remember that part of the voice mails?" When the nod wasn't forthcoming, he snarled again, "Remember?"

"I remember. I also remember you signed a contract." Rudi stood straight, trying to stare Kurt down from a three-inch height advantage. Hopeless against righteous fury.

"I did, which you are going to nullify, to keep us healthy and happy. Because—" The toothy not-smile Kurt gave him would have frightened wolves. "If our health and happiness fail because of you, I forget to reset the post dates on a whole bunch of blog posts that contain a whole bunch of interesting information that came out of that computer right there." He pointed at the monitor on the desk. "Years of information. A boatload of people, starting with Cassandra Rancier and ending with the man who controls this mountain will be very unhappy with you."

Rudi blanched and sat back against the desk, shaken to the core.

Egon glanced at me, taken totally aback by this side of Kurt. I shrugged, trying to say, "Don't mess with the man," with my shoulders. Suddenly all the typing in the night made sense.

"And to prevent that, all you have to do is tear up that contract and wish me well in the rest of my life. Which you are going to do right now, aren't you?" Kurt prodded Rudi's shoulder with an angry forefinger.

"Yes, certainly." Rudi glanced fearfully over his shoulder at Kurt as he went into the other room and opened a drawer. While Kurt followed him to the doorway, I grabbed the gun off the desk and slipped it into my pocket. If Rudi changed his mind, there was no point in making it easy for him.

He returned with a few sheets of paper. "Here, take it."

Kurt stepped backward into the main room, examining the paperwork before ripping it into dozens of shreds that he thrust in his pocket.

"This is all you want? To be released and left alone?" Rudi looked at me and Egon with uncertainty.

"Almost." Kurt zipped the pocket closed over the shreds. "I want our pal Egon to get the job that he thought he was getting. That he wants and I don't. Aren't you the lucky man, Rudi? You don't have to do without staff for a moment, and Egon here is anxious to shake his moneymaker for you."

"Fine, fine." Rudi couldn't agree fast enough. Egon relaxed, and why shouldn't he? Things were going his way.

"And." Kurt stopped, making Rudi look at him with some alarm. "I want to know why you hired me. Why you thought I'd do this at all. You sure didn't ask."

"I told you. You came well recommended. Glowingly recommended. What a mistake." Rudi looked ready to spit.

Kurt swallowed hard. "Who said it? And what exactly did they say?"

Rudi lifted one corner of his mouth—his next words could be a weapon. "Ah, it was a client of mine, Steven Shaffer. His words were, and I quote as best I can, 'Kurt Carlson will fuck anyone, anywhere, anytime.'"

The words took Kurt like a punch to the gut. "He said that."

I stepped up behind him. Half the mess these last few days had been caused by me not knowing the whole story. There had to be more than that to this bald statement, so I placed my hand on his shoulder and squeezed softly. Kurt shouldn't think I would make the same mistake twice, even in the teeth of this accusation.

Rudi smirked. "He was quoting his son, I believe." His knowing eyes dared me to react.

"Benji said that." Kurt swayed under my hand; I put my other hand on his other shoulder and pulled him back against my chest. Hearing the words and Kurt's acknowledgement was making me ill, but that would have to wait until we were done with Rudi, and Rudi was cruising for a bruising. My lover looked over his shoulder to catch my eye. "Yosemite."

"Oh. That." I made the words as nonchalant as possible. I already knew the story of the sex on the rock wall, and more to the point, I knew how badly it had hurt Kurt to be rejected afterward. He'd been more than half-afraid I'd do the same, five months ago. "Benji is old news, and a fool besides, Rudi. I wouldn't believe him if he said Colorado is cold in the winter." Kurt straightened under my hands. "Are we done here now, Kurt?"

"Just about. Congrats on the new job, Egon." He turned to go, but I had one last thing to say.

"Rudi. Believe everything he said." I gave him two seconds to digest that and then doubled him over with my fist to his belly. He fell writhing to the floor.

"I was gonna do that," Kurt reproved me mildly.

"Eh. My turn to clean up the mess." I pulled him over into a one-armed hug. "Let's get out of here."

TWENTY-NINE

Leaving our skis and boots in my locker at the staff hut let us wear our normal boots home. The ride on the shuttle was strange. I had so much to say and no desire to say it in front of the crowds returning from work on the mountain. The big advantage was that the shuttle was so full I got to stand pressed against Kurt's back, though millimeters, and sometimes nothing, kept other people from pressing against us.

Chelsea caught us halfway down the hallway. "Hi, guys! I was just looking for you!" I barely recognized her from the other night at McTavish's, but recalled seeing her strawberry-blonde curls nestled against Marty's shoulder. "I left a note on your door."

"Why? What did we do this time?" Kurt asked wearily.

"Rough day? Hey, I just wanted to find out if you guys had plans for tomorrow, or if you wanted to join us. It's a lot of the crew you've already met." Her wide, blue eyes had nothing but welcome in them, something Kurt and I hadn't been encountering a lot lately.

We looked at each other, trying to recall what was special about tomorrow. "I'm working," I said.

"We all are. Thanksgiving is always a busy day in a resort. We won't meet until around seven for dinner. I'm cooking the turkey now, because I've got classes all afternoon, and it will be out of the oven at midnight if I don't plan ahead. Do join us," she offered.

"Do you want us to bring something?" Kurt asked. "I'm off. I can take care of it."

Thanksgiving! How had we lost track so badly of the time? Oh, yeah....

"You are?" Chelsea was surprised, and then tried to hide it.

"Actually, I am unemployed. Temporarily, I hope, but tomorrow is mine. Is there something no one has volunteered for yet?" Kurt knitted his brows. Supplies might be a problem.

"No one's mentioned sweet potatoes." Chelsea paused. "Bring plates and silverware for yourself, that's the one thing we don't have enough of to go around, and plan to balance your plate on your lap. Marty and I are pretty casual with a group this big."

"We'll be there, Chelsea, and thanks." Kurt had already declared himself, so I'd just make it official. We had plenty to be thankful for, but a feast hadn't been on the radar. It would be good to have some time alone and good to spend some with friends.

"We're in 110, downstairs. And don't anybody give away the score on the Lions game, we're recording it to watch later," she advised us.

"What's to give away? Opposing team, big score, Lions, little score." I'd broken my heart on Lions football for years.

"The spread is the mystery, when you put it that way. And

they could surprise us, you never know." She smiled at us and started to leave. "It'll be a good time."

"Hey, Chelsea," I called her back. "Have you talked with Marty this afternoon?"

"No, why?" She stopped, puzzled.

"It's just...." How did I say this without admitting to knowledge I should not have? "Something pretty ghastly happened today. Be extra sweet to him, okay?"

"Okay. I guess you can't really talk about it, huh?" She gave me a searching look. She probably knew exactly where he was supposed to be and what he planned to do. The gears were visibly turning in her head. "What about Mark?"

"Him too." We were talking in code, but everyone was on the same page.

"Great. There isn't anyone who's especially sweet to him right now, but we'll try to take care of him." She sighed. "Thanks for the warning."

Once inside our apartment, we shed parkas and layers, though Kurt dug a few things out of a pocket before dropping the jacket where he stood. The gun I'd lifted from Rudi hit the floor with a muffled thud when I dropped my ski pants. I'd need to do something about that thing. Clothing hit the floor right and left. No wonder Kurt's socks led a life of their own; mine could start traveling at this rate.

The couch groaned when I threw myself flat against the cushions. "What a day. Come here." I held out my arms to him.

"Still one thing to do before I collapse." Kurt sat down with his butt against my waist. I let my hand drop into his lap, but didn't try to distract him when he started to poke numbers from a business card into his phone.

"Charles Lewis, please." Kurt leaned down so I could hear the call too. "Great. This is Kurt Carlson."

"Kurt! How'd you get my cell number? I didn't give it to you the other night." The voice on the other end was booming, somehow familiar, and not entirely friendly.

"James Underwood told me to call you. I didn't put it together with Charlie from McTavish's until just now." He looked perplexed.

"And why would James Underwood tell Alpenschlössl to give poor old Charlie a call?"

"Because he likes my teaching, he thinks you should offer me a job, and because I'm not Alpenschlössl. Never was, the way you mean it. I gave Rudi the boot." Charlie the gossip columnist could share that with the mountain all he liked.

"Did you now? I can only hope that was literal as well as figurative." He chuckled.

"No, though Jake did punch him." Great, now Charlie the gossip columnist could share that with the mountain too.

"Couldn't happen to a nicer guy. So, I should offer you a job? You turned me down the first time."

"Chalk it up to youth, foolishness, and because you didn't offer me the same princely sum that you're going to offer me this time." Kurt dropped one eyelid at me.

"I am?"

"Yes, you are. Because you are going to have requests for moguls and racing instruction by tomorrow, if you haven't already, and I don't think you read far enough back on my résumé."

"I recall one season teaching and patrolling at Breckenridge, two seasons teaching and patrolling at Jackson's Hole, what did I miss?"

"The important bits, like a full ride ski scholarship from the University of Colorado and two seasons on the US Ski Team. Little things that might mean I really know the skills you need me to teach." Whoa, that impressed me, though I was going to make him pay for giving me shit about the granola life at CU at Boulder when he'd gone there himself.

"CU, huh. Okay, you might be right about the skills part."

"I am. And the rest. So, what about it?" Kurt's words were lighthearted, but his face didn't match.

"As it happens, I've already talked to Mr. Underwood. Is this princely enough for you?" Charlie named a figure.

"Well...." Kurt pretended to consider it, while pumping his fist in the air. "It doesn't quite match my Alpenschlössl pay, but as long as I get to keep my pants on, it will do."

"You better damned well keep your pants on while you're on my time, Carlson." Good thing Charlie couldn't see Kurt leaning back and kicking his feet in excitement in his long johns. I did the happy dance on my back too, until I fetched Kurt a knee in the shoulder and had to settle down. "Start Friday. Be there early to fill out the paperwork."

"I'll see you then. Happy Thanksgiving, Charlie." Kurt hung up and then fell over on me, wriggling like a puppy. "That was easier than I thought it was going to be, Jake! He went for it, just like that!" He kissed me hard, and I grabbed his ass for glee.

"All right! That was great!"

"And all because little kids like you."

I poked him under the arms. "I hardly think that's the only reason, Kurt."

"Maybe not." He poked me back and then nestled on top of me and lay still. "It's been a rough couple of days, Jake. Really glad that's over."

There was still one looming disaster. I could keep quiet and Kurt might never know—but I'd know. "Uh, Kurt. One last thing."

His lifted eyebrows tickled my cheek. "Oh?"

"That bit where Mark said it never happened and I was never there—I was and it did."

"Meaning what?" He sounded tired.

"After the avalanche. Kurt, I wasn't kidding about him saving me. He got me off the slab and into the trees, and hung onto me so the avalanche vest would protect me too." I didn't want to hurt him, but I wanted him to hear this from me, just the way I'd heard about Benji from him.

"He hung on tightly, you mean."

"We both hung on; it was pretty scary. And when it was done, it was pretty damned good to be alive."

"So good that you...."

"Kissed him. I'm sorry, Kurt, but I kissed him." Should I even be holding him while I confessed this?

"I see." Kurt lifted a hand to my face and ran his thumb down my jaw. "So how did he taste?"

How could he be so mild about this? "Pretty good at first, but then he didn't taste like you, and I got scared that you'd been caught, so I had to go look for you." I caught his hand and pressed it against my cheek.

"Planning to do it again?" His voice was still soft.

"No. I wasn't planning to do it the first time."

"I suppose surviving an avalanche could be considered extenuating circumstances. We both know about being glad to be alive." He went back to stroking my jaw. "I know how Mark feels about you, and I can't argue with his taste in men. He did keep you safe, so I guess I won't begrudge him the one kiss." One more caress on my jaw, and then he was poised over me, staring down with slightly crazed eyes. "*Just don't ever do it again!*"

"I won't, Kurt." I pulled him back down on top of me, and

he let me, settling back into my arms. "I don't want anyone but you."

"Good. And don't pull a Benji on him, either."

"What's that?"

"Don't turn your back on him because of what happened. Just let it go. You said it yourself, a guy needs friends, and he's going to need them more than most after today. You and Marty are the only ones he'll be able to talk to about it, except maybe me. Maybe. But he won't dare tell anyone else, and no one will understand except for someone who was there."

"I won't." Friendship I was good on, though I didn't know if Mark would be. Kurt really was understanding.

"But no kissing or anything else!" Kurt was over me again, shouting.

"Right. I won't. Easy, Kurt." Once more I pulled him down to my chest and patted him to quiet. "I won't. Only you." Make that, Kurt was understanding and possessive. Good. Because I was his.

Everything we needed to say was getting said just now with small touches, gentle caresses. He was a welcome weight on top of me, a warm blanket against the world. I played with his shoulder, keeping my other hand still since it lay right over the bruise Egon had left. Which made me wonder… "Why did you need to get Egon involved?"

"I needed him to be my replacement, not Ulf's. Rudi would have fought a lot harder if he'd known he needed two people and not just one. Did you know Egon is supporting his family in Bulgaria? That's why he was so angry at getting passed over."

I didn't want to give up my perception of Egon as a complete jerk, but this was something to think about.

Something more to think about.

We lay together silently, with all the turmoil in my head,

and maybe in his. I wanted to say a thousand things, all at once, and couldn't pick one to say first lest the others seem the less important. Things about being careful, that I was glad he was alive, that I was proud of him for being who and what he was, and all of the wonderful things those were. That I was glad he chose to be with me. That I stood amazed at how he'd solved the Alpenschlössl problem without hurting people we liked. That he could forgive me, and that he could be strong enough to stick around while I grew strong enough to forgive him for something that didn't need forgiveness in the end. I needed, desperately, a way to tell him all that, but there was just no way to begin.

But there was. Using words that I'd shied away from because I didn't want them to mean the wrong thing when I used them. But if I said them now, they'd mean everything, and I could explain the details in small chunks. This time, they'd be the right words.

He broke the silence. "Tomorrow is Thanksgiving. We have a lot to be thankful for."

"We do." I squeezed him tighter and rubbed my cheek against his hair. "Starting with being together."

"Especially that." He sighed and seemed to get a little flatter against me.

"Especially that." I tipped his face up to mine and kissed him gently. "You matter more to me than anyone in the world. Kurt, I…." The words stuck, making me clear my throat. "I love you, Kurt."

"Oh, Jake." He raised up over me again, but close this time, close enough for kisses. "Jake, I…." He trailed off, leaving my chest hollow as I waited to hear what he thought of this. "Jake, I… I love you too."

Then he bent to kiss me, and Thanksgiving started.

ABOUT THE AUTHOR

P.D. Singer lives in Colorado with her slightly bemused husband, one proto-adult, and twelve pounds of cats. She's a big believer in research, firsthand if possible, so the reader can be quite certain Pam has skied down a mountain face first, been stepped on by rodeo horses, acquired a potato burn or two, and will never, ever, write a novel that includes skydiving.

When not writing, playing her fiddle, or skiing, she can be found with a book in hand.

Follow the adventures at Pam's website.

Keep current with Pam and the Rocky Ridge gang by joining the newsletter.

ALSO BY P.D. SINGER

Fire on the Mountain

Fall Down the Mountain

Blood on the Mountain

Return to the Mountain

Coming Out From the Mountains (coming soon)

Running to Him

Spokes

The Rare Event

A New Man

Diving Deep

Concierge Service

A TASTE OF FALL DOWN THE MOUNTAIN

PROLOGUE (MARK AND ALLAN)

The snow beneath my skis shattered. Cracks opened below me —the solid snowpack disintegrated and slid. Snow would crash down the mountain, carrying away anything, everything in its path. Unimaginable tons would roar down the chute where two peaks met. Only the bedrock of the mountains could withstand the avalanche. Nothing on the surface would defy it, certainly not puny specks of humans.

I hurtled toward the two skiers, bellowing, "Get off the slab! Get off the slab!" They weren't moving fast enough. My training screamed *Get away! Leave them both!* My heart said *No!* but I could only save one. Acting before I could think, I swooped to the side, catching one man. He stayed on his feet, else I'd have to leave him. Or die with him, if we didn't reach the trees.

My survival vest would inflate into a big red ruff. I might live if the slide caught us. He wouldn't. It would keep me at the surface. Him, too, for a few seconds. The roaring maelstrom would tear us apart.

The mountain detonated before we reached the trees. White

spume hid the sky; the snowpack exploded in a deadly bellow. The hill fell apart beneath us.

We fought to reach higher ground. I lost my grip—the snow stole him from my hand. He screamed, tumbling downhill. The pounding of the avalanche drowned any words. I could only watch helplessly from the trees, yelling, "Take my hand!" My outstretched arm wasn't long enough. Fifteen arms wouldn't be long enough. The chaos swallowed him.

Did it last a minute? An hour? I couldn't tear my eyes from where he had been. The horror—eternal—I'd see his panicked face forever.

The mountain quieted. I sped to the faraway hillock in the snow, horribly certain of what I'd find. Like a compass needle to north, I skied straight to that mound, tearing the shovel off my belt. "Be alive!" I threw scoops of snow behind me. "Be alive!"

The snow, hard as concrete, came away in clumps as I dug. Finally, blond hair and a red jacket appeared—I dug faster and could finally brush the snow from his face. "Breathe!" I commanded. "I'll get you out!"

His eyes were open, but he was still. Too still. No breath. No movement. Kurt looked up sightlessly from the snow. I hadn't saved him after all.

"No!" I screamed to the uncaring mountain that threw my words back to me:"Nooooooo!"

Read the rest.

ALSO FROM ROCKY RIDGE BOOKS

The Diversion Series from Eden Winters

Diversion

Collusion

Corruption

Manipulation

Redemption

Reunion

Suspicion

Decision

The Wrestling Series from D.H. Starr

Wrestling With Desire

Wrestling with Love

Wrestling With Passion

Wrestling with Hope

The Dark Angels Series from Z. Allora

With Wings

Tied Together

Finally Fallen